Fragmented
Pieces

by

Mocha J.

Copyright © 2020 by Mocha J.

All rights reserved.
Published in the United States by Mocha J.

ISBN 978-0-578-85214-0

Editors: Shelia Jones and Cordero Lane
Cover Design: Byron Gillison

IN LOVING MEMORY OF MARY LOU JONES

Look Ma, I made it!

This is for you. Thank you for your kindness, devotion, and for your endless support. Thanks for always holding me down and loving me. You will always be in my heart!

Fragmented
Pieces

INTRODUCTION

Sitting in a crowded room and I still feel alone! I can hear all the noise around me, but I feel as if I'm the only one in the room. This room is a metaphor for my life. I am crowded in my own space! Giving of me freely to all of those around me, but no one is giving back. With all the things are going on in my life: My husband, my stepdaughter, my friends, and everyone else around m, and yet I still feel so alone. As I sit in this crowed room, I can feel everyone looking past me and all I can do is cry on the inside. When will this world see me? When will the people around me see the person that I truly am? When will I see myself as the beautiful creature that God created? I know that I can accomplish great things in life, but I can't get past me.

Learning to love myself is the hardest thing that I will ever have to do in my life! How can I truly love someone that I am in an intimate relationship with if I can't love me? Looking in the mirror every day I feel disgusted! I wish everyone could see me through my eyes so they can see the brokenness that lies deep within. I feel alone every day of my life and it has been this way since I was a little girl. Being away from my parents and being raised by others that treated me as if I didn't matter was hard on me and shaped my self-image.

No one knows that I feel this way but my husband. The one man that I thought I could talk to and would help me build myself only tore me down more. He made me feel as if I wasn't good enough, just like all the other men that came before him. When I'm alone with him he doesn't talk to me unless it's about his child. If I try to talk to him, I am unable to get his attention. The only time that I feel wanted is when we are having sex. Yeah that's right, sex, and even that is different. I can tell that when he is having sex with me, he is thinking of any other woman that he has been with. His touch is not the same anymore! His kiss is not the same anymore! Sometimes during sex, I just lie there and cry because I know that his heart doesn't belong to me anymore. We are both just holding on because we are too scared to let go. We have both become accustomed to each other but can't stand one another. Sometimes I watch him while he sleeps and wish he would die so I can be rich. Yeah, he's better off dead to me than alive. That shack that we lived in when we first got married was probably more depressing than my life.

I'm sorry I got off track; my life is hard yawl!

With all the new adventures that I am currently taking in my life, learning to love myself is my biggest challenge. At times I cry, and I don't know why I'm crying, I guess my soul needs a cleansing.

People looking in from the outside think that I got my shit together but if they only knew. I give my all to everyone especially the man that I love but he doesn't want me. I know you're probably thinking that if I am so miserable with my husband that I should just leave? Well as I said earlier, I can't just leave I love him, and I know that somewhere deep down inside that he loves me too.

CHAPTER 1

In my college days I tried all that I could to make myself feel whole by accepting things as they were and just being. I'm a beautiful caramel skinned woman and I stand 5 feet 9 inches tall. Oh yes, I am a tall drink of water as they say. Many of the guys would try and talk to me but after being hurt in high school I just couldn't deal with the drama that comes with relationships. There are some fine guys that were trying to talk to me, but I must stay focused on school and becoming a better me. Funny thing is I have been looking for myself since high school and I still haven't found myself.

Walking around campus I saw this guy and instantly my heart stopped. He was 6 feet 6 inches and fine dark chocolate. This wasn't my first time seeing him, but this was the first time my body reacted to his presence. I started having visions of what my life could be with him. He was my future and he didn't know it! I walked pass him hoping he would say something to me, but he ignored me, so I kept walking.

Four months later I saw him again in the student lounge. At that moment our eyes connected, and my breath caught, this man had an effect on me that no other man has ever had. He glided across the room to the table where I sat and he said, "Hey Beautiful" and I just giggled. My body was doing things that it has never done before. As he sat there and stared into my hazel eyes, I couldn't utter a sound. This man was good! I wondered if he had this effect on all the women that he encountered or was it just me that reacted this way.

His name was Derrick. He was from Florida and he was the star basketball player and yes, he was fine as hell. This man had charisma and an arrogance about himself that told me I should run. But I was so enthralled by this man that I wanted to get to know him more, hell I wanted to have his babies. Deep down I know that he was no good for me, but I wanted this man. Every good girl needs a bad boy!

After meeting Derrick in the lounge, we begin meeting once a week to have lunch and sometimes dinner. We talked about our past and the things that we wanted to accomplish in life.   There was something about him that made me feel safe and secure when I was with him. I told him my deepest darkest secrets as we got closer. He became my sounding board and I became his.

My mom warned me about him; she was that he was just too perfect. She felt that something was off with him and it just didn't feel right. Mom would call and check on me once a week, but she would always end the call with "Marie, I don't know about this Derrick guy, he just seems to perfect and there is no one that perfect but God". I would always brush off her comments because my mom was just jealous because she had never had a lasting relationship in her life. Her relationships always end quickly. They would all leave taking a piece of her heart and soul leaving her to search for the next man.

Later in my life I found out that instead of disregarding my mother's comments, I should have listened because it would have saved me a lot of heartache and pain.

Derrick and I would go to church and pray together. He would call me every morning before class and pray with me. Our relationship progressed quickly but I was extremely happy. Well at least I thought we were happy. I started hearing rumors of Derrick being with other females, but I didn't want to believe them. I would always ask him about the rumors, and he would always say that I was the only woman for him. Yeah, I know you are thinking that this girl is so naïve! I was naïve and believed everything that he told me because I had never been loved by a man like this. I had given my all to this man and he was everything that I wanted.

After all the rumors died down, I got a surprise visit from a girl named Regina. I've seen her around campus, but I have never had a reason to have a conversation with her. Derrick told me that she was the campus hoe and to stay away from her. So why is she standing here wanting to talk to me? We have nothing in common. When she came to my table, she said "Hi Marie, I would like to talk to you for a moment". I was taken aback. How did she know my name? How did she know me? I keep a low profile around campus because Derrick doesn't want the guys peeping me. I'm confused as to why she needs to talk to me. Let me stop staring and daydreaming and just ask the girl. "Hi Regina, is there something I can help you with?" Regina has this strange look on her face then she blurts out that she is pregnant by Derrick.

No! This can't be happening to me! Why did this girl come over to my table and flat out lie on Derrick? He would never touch anybody like her. I now sit here ready to slap the taste out of her lying ass mouth. How dare she come in here and lie on Derrick. He is a God-fearing man and would never cheat on me. Regina looks at me with her own disgust and states that Derrick really has you fooled. She lets me know that she was not the only other woman that he was dealing with. I was also told that they all know that I was his main chick and there was nothing that they could do about it. If they wanted him, they had to understand that he was never leaving me. Now I sit here wondering what type of women would be with a man like that, but I knew they were mistaken.

Derrick was a good man and he has already told me that women would do anything to break up our relationship because they didn't want to see us happy. I confronted Derrick later that night and he denied what Regina had told me. He reconfirmed that he would never date a woman like that. We prayed for all those women that were trying to come in between our love.

While around campus I watched for Regina. I believed everything that Derrick said but there was something in me that didn't feel right. I watch Regina for month! Derrick stayed close to me around campus to put on a united front to all those that doubted the love that he had for me. I knew that this man truly loved me.

I would later find out that he was only sticking close to me on campus because he was afraid that one of his women would seek me out again. Everything changed in our relationship when I saw Regina again. I heard that she had taken ill and left school for a semester. She is now back and so is her protruding belly. Maybe she had gotten pregnant while she was away from campus. I have this gut feeling again that something isn't right, but I am going to keep a watchful eye on Regina and Derrick.

When Derrick came home later that night, I informed him that I saw Regina around campus, and she was surely pregnant. The look on his face was as if he had seen a ghost. He started stuttering "yo-o-o-o-ou saw ah, ah who?

"Regina, Derrick don't act like you don't know her. You remember the girl that told me several months ago that she was carrying your child."

He says "Ah-ah-ah-ah where di-di-di-did you see her?"

"I-I-I-I thought sh-sh-sh-she left school?"

Now I'm sitting here trying to figure out why he has this dumb ass look on his face. I knew he was hiding something because the only time he stuttered was when he was lying.

"Wait one damn minute! Derrick is that baby yours?"

Now his dumb ass has gone mute.

"You hear me talking to you DERRICK! If you want to save your relationship you better come clean now or just walk out of my life".

"Come on Marie, why would you ask me such a stupid question"

"Derrick, I know something is up with you and this girl by your reaction to knowing that she was back."

"Marie, stop tripping."

"Derrick I'm not tripping, I just need the truth so I can go on with my life."

"Ok Marie, if you promise not to leave me, I will come clean about everything, but know I can't function in my life without you. These other women don't mean anything. You make my life complete. I apologize for everything that I am about to say to you"

"Derrick just tell me, I can't promise you that I will not leave you!"

"I did have sex with Regina, but it was only twice. You knew that I was a sexually active man before I met you and you are waiting until marriage. Because you would not have sex with me, I had to seek other means. That doesn't mean that I love you any less, it just means that I had to take care of the desires I have as a man. I have needs that you were not willing to handle so what did you expect me to do?

If you would have been having sex with me, I would have never gone to that girl!"

"So you're blaming your infidelity on me? Really Derrick! I can't deal with you right now, I'm leaving! You and Regina have a nice life together."

"No Marie, don't leave me!"

I'm sorry! I promise this will never happen again".

As I walked away I looked back at him standing there crying and my heart broke. I was walking out on the love of my life. My life will never be the same!

CHAPTER 2

Marie

Derrick constantly called, came by and sent flowers, and each time ignored him. My heart sank knowing that I had lost the only man that I ever loved. I spent many nights just crying and praying asking God where I went wrong. Was it really my fault that Derrick cheated on me? Why did I have to be such a prude? This is my final year in college, and I am a big girl why am I acting so childish? I keep thinking that I can't let this man go.

I spoke with my mother yesterday hoping that she for once would be a mother and understand what I was going through. But no, not Alice, she had to try and rub it in my face and say I told you so. She was so miserable in her own life that she was happy to see that a man had done me like all men had done her. I now realize that we will never have the mother/daughter relationship that I have always wanted. As of today; I decided to never discuss my relationship issues with her.

It has now been five months and close to graduation and I have decided that I am finally ok to just be me and live my life. Life without Derrick was hard but I was maintaining. He was the only true family that I had; my mother wasn't interested in my college success. My father was someone that I knew of, but he was never a part of my life. Some days I feel so lonely without him in my life, but I have to be strong. Every day I have to say, "God give me strength".

One day I was out walking around campus enjoying my day and I saw Regina. She was glowing! I never took the time to really look at the girl. I walked up to her and asked if she was ok. This time she was taken aback because I came to her. She apologized for her part in the breakup of Derrick and me. She wanted me to know that she was having a little girl and that she would not be a problem if Derrick and I chose to work our relationship out. I sat there in shock because I was never planning on getting back with him.

It was true that I still loved him, but could I truly forgive him for the hurt and pain that he put me through?

Seeing Derrick brought back memories that I couldn't shake. After all this time, I bumped into him. I had been avoiding him like the plague! Somehow today we have run into each other. Life with him was good but I'm standing here thinking that I need this man in my life. Seeing him made feelings rush back to the surface that I had suppressed. Looking at this man I know that I truly love him and maybe I can forgive him.

He walks up to me and speaks. "Hi Marie, its good running into you today, I have really missed seeing you every day.

"Hi Derrick", I say. Trying to suppress my feelings for him.

"Marie, can I talk to you for a moment?"

"What is it that you need to talk about?"

"Us."

"Us? There is no us the last time I checked. You messed 'US' up Derrick!"

"Come on Marie! Don't be like that; I am still in love with you."

"Fine Derrick we can talk but, I'm only giving you five minutes."

"Five minutes? Come on Marie, our relationship will take more time than that."

"Five minutes is all you get Derrick! Take it or leave it."

"Ok, Marie! Well first off I wanted to let you know how beautiful you look today."

"Come on Derrick, let's get this over with!"

"Well Marie, I just want you to know that my life has been miserable without you. There is no other woman in this world that can ever take your place. You were made for me as I was made for you! I can't sleep without knowing that you are mine. I don't want to feel that I have lost you. You are a big part of my life. You are my hope and my future! You're my queen! I love you Marie and I am sorry for everything that I have done to make you lose faith in me, in us."

"Derrick as I have told you before, I accept your apology and wish you success in your life. I just ask that you be a great father to Regina's little girl."

"Marie, do you hear what I am trying to tell you?"

As I stand there with tears in my eyes looking at the man that I thought I would spend the rest of my life with my heart is softening toward him. I really love this man. The bible has taught us to forgive and move on; not forgiving him is causing me pain.

CHAPTER 3

Now years later we sit in this two-bedroom shack and the man that I thought my husband was, is only an illusion. Before we got married, he wooed me. I mean this man showed this little country girl things that I had never seen before.   All my first experiences were with this man. Now this man has shown me the devil he truly is.

After our first year of marriage I found out about Diane. She was all that I wasn't and probably more. She was an executive at a major ad Agency with major confidence, where I was a stay at home wife with a broken self-image.

I never let my husband know that I knew about Diane and just attempted to play big girl and step my game up. However, no matter what I did it was never enough for him. I mean anything this man ask for, whether it be in the bedroom, the house, the kitchen, and I mean anything I did just to keep him home.

I remember this one time he told me he wanted me to be a little freakier in the bedroom. So, I went out and bought a pair of seven-inch black stiletto heels, a negligee, and a red wig. He just didn't know what I had waiting on him when he got home. Right before Derrick's eyes I turned into Pinky the porn star. I stripped for him to the song shut it down by Drake and then I fucked and sucked this nigga for three hours straight. I did shit that I never thought I could or would even do to this ungrateful man. After our night of fun, he laid in bed for about an hour until I drifted off into a light sleep. He then left me there to go be with his "FAMILY".

Derrick was treating me like his whore and not his wife. It is hard being married to a man and feeling like his side chick instead of his wife.

Now I know that you are thinking that I should have left him then, but I didn't. I loved this man and thought that he would have a short affair, but this affair lasted fifteen years. Diane knew he was married, and he had told her all these details about me, for what I don't know. She didn't even need to know my name, but she knew where we lived, that I didn't have a job, hell she even knew what type of car I drove. I've always wondered why she needed to know so much information about me. Well I did some digging and found out that this woman had to audacity to have a son. Derrick had a family that I knew nothing about. That's why he was always gone. But what little miss Dianne didn't know was he was cheating on both of us. Yeah you heard me right. He was having an affair with a lady named Kami.

But it was something about Derrick that made me stay with his lying cheating ass; or was it my insecurity. Whatever it was I was there, and I was going to ride this thing out until the wheels fell off. When I got married it was for better or worse, for richer or poor, until death do us part. Well we are both still alive and that's only because I'm too pretty to go to jail. Yeah if I wasn't scared of jail and some big cock strong woman taking my cookies, I would have killed his ass after the first year of marriage. Ok, I digress! Derrick is a sweet and gentle guy he just has a wayward dick!

Derrick and I have had some pretty good times together, but all this other drama he keeps bringing in our lives, has broken me down so much, that I don't see the powerful queen that I am. I feel like a gutter rat at times, accepting the little crumbs of a relationship that this man has laid out for me. Life can be crazy sometimes, but we must deal with the cards that has been laid out for us. I just have to continue to work on our union, but it is hard when you can't trust a word that comes out of his mouth. He has turned me into this bitter black woman that he hates. He says I have changed since we got together; but won't accept the fact that he is the reason for my change.

Hell, I feel if he can do it, his bitch ass better believe that I can do it better! Yes; can you believe it my fat depressed ass have thought about cheating? But what good would that do! I'll still be a miserable fat bitch crying over a no-good nigga, so I sit and wait and pray for him to do better.

CHAPTER 4

I know that everyone hates on me right about now, but you can't judge me by what you've heard. I'm really a good guy, I just have a few issues and pussy is one of them. I love Marie and I can't see my life without her, however, she has let herself go. She walks around looking sloppy and depressed all the time so what am I supposed to do as a man!

I'm a good-looking man and if women want me then they can have me as long as they can keep their damn mouth shut. I never hide from any woman the fact that I am married. They know that I am not leaving my wife, and this is only a fuckship; nothing more. The minute these women get clingy I have to let them go. God didn't bless me to look like this and with a dick like this to only be with one woman. If my father was able to take care of two household and his women on the side, why can't I?

Growing up I was a part of the second family that my father had. When my father Dominic met my mother, he had already been married to April for over ten years. April was a little older than my father and she had difficulties having children. After being married for ten years she finally got pregnant with a little girl that they later named Miracle. Yeah, I know that it's a corny name, but her mother felt that she was a gift from God. What she didn't know was that Dominic was planning on leaving her because she was barren. Having Miracle changed Dominic's plans. He loved April and he finally got what he wanted, a little girl that he could give the world to.

Now when my father Dominic met my mother, she was young and entering her sophomore year at college. My mother was from a small town in Louisiana, she was never allowed to date. When she met my father, he swept her off her feet.

Eventually he bought them a little quaint house near the college campus so she could finish school. He never told her that he was married. By the time she found out, she was already pregnant with me. See, my father was a business man and traveled a lot, so she would have never suspected that he had another family. He hid this very well.

Unfortunately, April did not know about my mother. By the time I turned five my mother was fed up with being the other woman. One day while out grocery shopping my mother bumped into April "by accident". My mother was tired of living a lie and she wanted Dominic to herself.   Miracle and I looked like we should be twins but of course we had different mothers.

As they were walking in the aisle at the local farmers market, my mother bumped into April.

"Oh I'm sorry, I didn't see you there."

"It's ok, accidents happen."

"What a pretty little girl you have there". "What's your name sweetie?"

My big sister just looked at her but didn't respond.

April says "I'm sorry she is a little shy and doesn't like to talk to strangers."

This comment from April pissed my mother off.

"Well April, I'm really not a stranger."

"Oh, have we met somewhere before? I don't remember ever meeting you. If I have, I'm sorry I don't remember."

"Well technically you have never met me, I'm Olivia and we share the same man."

"Olivia! I don't know who the hell you are nor do I care, but if you wanted to talk to me you should have come to me woman to woman! I guess that you are another one of Dominic 's tramps huh! He must have given you a title because you are a bold little bitch aren't you!'

This really pissed my mother off more because she didn't get the response from April that she was expecting.

"So, April now that you know who I am let me introduce you to my son, Derrick! Yes, he is Dominic's son! I gave him what a real woman could give him. It took you many years to produce one child. I have given him a son and I am currently pregnant with his second son while you're only offering him some dried out, tainted ovaries. If I was you, I would leave him and let him be with his family. Oh, but don't worry I will make sure that you and your daughter are taken care of."

"Ms. Olivia, hoe, homewrecker, or whatever you would like to be called please do your bidding somewhere else. If Dominic truly wanted, you to be a family he would have left me when he got you pregnant. He would have also left me when he found out that these poor old tainted ovaries couldn't produce children as you say. Now that you know about my daughter make sure he tells you about the son that I am pregnant with. Yes, pick your face up his wife is giving him the only son that will carry his last name. Have a great day!'

My mother left the store with her feelings hurt that day because my father told her that it was over with him and his wife. She believed every lie that he had ever told her. That night he came to the house and beat my mother for causing problems with his family. It hurt me so bad to sit there and watch my mother hurt and bruised over a man that was not hers. I vowed that day that I would be nothing like this man!

My father continued to live a double life and both women accepted it. April lived her life with her two children and my mother did the same. Dominic divided his time between both houses, but he was still not satisfied and had multiple women in several locations. All these women understood their relationship with him and never overstepped their boundaries.

Now today I am the man that my father was just not the abuser. Let me take that back, I am an abuser, just not the physical type. I have been verbally abusive and mentally abusive to Marie all in the name of love.

Marie was and still is my world, but just like my father her inability to give me children has cause me to find a woman that could. She has been the perfect stepmother to my daughter with Regina and her relationship with Regina even surprised me. She has accepted Regina and is the only one in our relationship that has communication with her. Of course, I would talk to her but she doesn't want to have anything to do with me.

Now Diane is my equal and I love her. With her, everything is just so much easier. Diane is waiting on me to divorce Marie, but I have no plans on doing so. Diane gave me a son, Derrick Jr., I'm very proud to be a father and I plan to be in his life. Just like my father I will be the perfect man in both my families.

As I lay here in the bed with Diane, I think about my life with Marie. Marie is awesome in bed and is the perfect wife, but she can never be the mother of my children. She has let herself go and now all she does is nag about everything. She used to be so beautiful and powerful now she looks fat and dumpy. Diane is everything that a man of my stature would want. She is petite, caramel skin, long flowing hair and has the body of a goddess but the sex is mediocre. I am with her not only because of her beauty but because she challenges me, and she stimulates my mind.

Diane is the woman that Marie used to be. I think that I am falling in love with her, I just can't fall out of love with Marie. Don't get me wrong, Marie is a good woman and she had a lot going on for herself and I don't have to worry about her ever leaving me or even cheating on me. I've always liked the fact that Marie is a good Christian girl and would always be there for me. There are times that I think that she is getting fed up with my bullshit, but she hasn't left yet. As long as I take care of home and throw some money her way, she'll be ok.

CHAPTER 5

I am getting fed up with the bullshit Derrick is putting me through. He thinks he can treat me any kind of way. Today as I look in the mirror, I realize that I have let myself go. It is time to get healthy and get back to the queen I am. My first task of the day is to start looking for a job and get myself a gym membership.

I can no longer allow Derrick to treat me like 'the other woman' when I should be the only woman in his life. I have spent too much of my life chasing a man who doesn't want me. Diane, Kami, or any other woman can have his ass.

I pick up the phone to call the two people who won't say 'I told you so' but will have my back. It's funny how life has a way of working itself out; I called Regina. Yes, I called Regina, the one Derrick cheated on me with in college. Being that she is the mother of his child, we became very good friends over the years.

I also called Miracle, Derrick's sister. Miracle and I have always been close since the first day we met. We have a true sisterhood. She hates the way her brother treats me because it reminds her of the relationship between her father and mother. Although her parents had a toxic relationship, they loved each other and made it work for them.

The three of us met for lunch at the local bar. I finally broke down and told the ladies everything that was going on in my life. The look on their faces scared the hell out of me. Regina chimed in and said, "Oh no Marie. I knew that Derrick was a dog, but I didn't know that he was that low down. I know how we met was not good, but it was the best thing that ever happened to me."

Miracle said, "Marie you are my sister and I love you dearly. Growing up, I watched the light dim in my mother's eyes. I have been watching the light dim in yours also. You must fight, Marie! Get your fire back! Regina and I are here to help you in any way that we can.".

"As I sit here in tears, I am happy for the true sisterhood that I have found with you two ladies."

"Aww, now stop with all of this mushy stuff and let's plan your escape from my brother."

"Miracle you act like I am escaping from jail!"

"No, not jail but it was the insane asylum, because your ass had to be crazy as hell to stay with my brother's doggish ass. And we can start by finding you a good man."

"No, Miracle I am not ready to be with another man right now."

"Ok. Marie and Miracle let's make these plans. The first plan is to do something with that hair of yours."

"What's wrong with my hair Regina?"

"What's NOT wrong Marie?"

"Miracle, while I am at the beauty shop with Marie can you go out and buy her a few outfits. And don't get her the usual frumpy outfits that she wears."

"Don't worry Regina we will make her hot again."

"Really? You two heifers are talking about me as if I am not here. I don't look that bad! Remember I am the only woman at this table with a man!"

And they both said in unison, "I'm glad I am single if I have to have a man like Derrick."

"Ok, ladies let's get to work."

Before I knew it, I was sitting in the chair at the salon excited to see the new me. Regina sat me in the chair and told the beautician to have his way with me. I felt like I was on one of those makeover shows because they wouldn't let me look at myself. As I waited on the beautician to complete my makeover, I anticipated the beauty I had hidden for so many years. As my makeup was being applied, Miracle came in with my dress. The girls were discussing which once is better for me.

Once they had the outfit picked out with the perfect shoes, they sent me to the dressing room to get ready. I did a once over in the mirror and I don't recognize the woman I saw. She looked familiar, but I had not seen this woman in years. I couldn't wait to see what they have planned next.

When I stepped out of the dressing area, all eyes were on me! The beautician, Alexis, was the first to comment and everyone else chimed in. It wasn't until the man delivering the water at the salon said, "damn" that I opened my eyes. I had to look around the room to see who the hell he was talking to. The water guy was fine and made me think that maybe I do need to start searching for another man. I don't want to be in a relationship anytime soon, but I do need a man to crack my back every now and again.

I stood up straight and walked over to get me a glass of water. I made sure to bend over so he could see all the heavenly curves I've been blessed with.

Damn, as I get closer, he looks a little younger but there is nothing wrong with letting him observe all my beauty.

Once he left, I realized I was holding my breath the entire time. It's a good thing that I didn't pass out while trying to be cute. Everyone was staring at me and I turned and said 'What? Damn a bitch can't observe the beauty of a man"?

Regina and Miracle were happy to see me smiling again. Then they informed me that I had a dinner date tonight with Derrick. I looked at them both strange because they are supposed to help me get over him not bring me closer to him. But it would be a good thing for him to see what he had because after today he will be losing me.

Dinner was very romantic but hard for me to get through it without pouring my soul out to Derrick. Every time I look at him, I remember just how much

I love him, then I remember what a dog he is. He is sitting here smiling now but he never noticed the luggage that was sitting outside the front door.

Derrick finally says something, and it makes me want to throw this plate of food in his face.

"Marie, baby, you are looking so beautiful tonight! What happened to you and why are you dressed like that? This is not the woman that I trained you to be".

I want to cry so badly but my eye makeup looked so good and I don't want to mess it up. Plus, Derrick is used to seeing that weak and meek woman that he thought he trained.

What the hell you mean "trained" Derrick? You didn't train me. I was the woman that I thought you needed me to be while we were married but you took advantaged of my kindness. And the sad part is that I let you"!

"You heard me right Marie. I trained you and you have been a good little woman. Now that you are playing dress up tonight you think you can talk to me any kind of way. I think not! You are the woman you are because of me. Everything that you have is because of me! You need to always remember MARIE that you are nothing without me and I mean nothing"!

Really Derrick, is that how you really feel about me? The one that you were so in love with, the one that you have treated like a side bitch since college. The sad part is that I allowed you to treat me like that. But not anymore brother, I have awakened from this nightmare of a marriage and I see the light. My future is good and there is no place for you in my future".

"HAHAHAHA, Marie I see that you been hanging with Miracle and Regina again! I keep telling you that Regina is not your friend. How can you be friends with a woman that not only wanted but had a baby by your man? And Miracle is a bitter bitch!"

DERRICK! How dare you talk about either of them like that?   Regina and I are friends because of a mistake that she made with your lying, cheating ass. She didn't know about me just as I didn't know about her, so thank you for bringing her into my life. That's the only good thing that you have done for me since we have been together. I have put up with your bullshit for way too long and it is time to end this sham of a marriage".

"What do you mean sham? Marie, we have had a damn good marriage and you are just being ungrateful right now"!

"Derrick let's just finish dinner and we can talk about this another time. I just wanted to show you just what a good woman you had."

Derrick stood up and walked over to me, he offered his hand to help me up out of the chair. As he attempted to walk to the stairs to go up to what use to be his bedroom we stopped at the door and I opened it for him.

Derrick looked at me dumbfounded and confused. "Oh, Derrick there Is no need to look like that. I am tired of your bullshit and I no longer want to be married to you".

"Come on Marie! I love you! We are supposed to be together until death do us part."

I look at Derrick and he looks as if he wanted to cry. I'm thinking to myself this fool betta not let a tear drop. As I am thinking this, a tear falls from his eye and I felt my heart break, but I must stay strong. Derrick you have to leave now!

"I'm not going anywhere! This is my house and I have rights to be here!"

Rights! You lost your rights when you left me that night to go be with Diane.

"Is this what this is about Diane?"

"Marie she is the mother of my child and I can't just leave her I have no choice but to be with her."

"Oh, Derrick you have a choice and you made that choice after I pulled out all of my best shit to fuck you in to submission and you left our bed to go be with her."

"Marie, I tried to explain to you that my son was sick, and I had to go to him"

"Derrick you are so full of shit"!

"Come on Marie, I love you and I promise if you stay with me, I will leave Diane and only take care of Derrick Jr."

"I guess you're a comedian now because the shit you are saying now you don't even believe yourself."

"Marie, I promise to do right by you just don't leave me."

Derrick let the tears flow and he hugged me. The fool had the nerve to try and kiss me. I don't think so! I had to let him know that the only thing that he will be kissing is my ass!

"Bye Derrick, I hate that you were not a different person because I truly was in love with you. You were my all and there was nothing that I wouldn't have done from you. You changed me and it wasn't for the better and I need to get the old me back. I am stronger now because I am letting you go! Have a wonderful life with Diane and Kami!"

"Kami, Marie who the hell is Kami!"

Derrick don't act like you don't know who she is I just hope that Diane finds out the person that you are.

"Don't try to attack my character Marie! I'm a good man and I take care of what's mine. You have not worked since we have gotten married. You drive a nice car, live in a nice house and can buy anything that you desire to buy, and you are being ungrateful."

"Again Derrick, you have a good life. Yes, I know about Kami, she is a stripper that you are fucking and she is too young and naïve to know what type of man that you really are. She is blinded by the

money and all the fine things that you are flashing.
I feel sorry for the poor girl."

"Marie, my life can't go on without you"

"You've been doing just fine Derrick just keep being
who you are. You have your new family with Diane,
she can now be happy to have you full time now."

"I'll go for now; but you'll be sorry.

CHAPTER 6

I am not sure why you are looking at me like that. Derrick's marriage was over when I got with him. That bitch Marie just wouldn't give him a divorce. He travels so much, and he stays with me when he can, so I don't know why she is holding on to something that has been over a long time ago.   If she would have taken care of her husband, she wouldn't have lost him.

I met Derrick at a time in my life when I was down and had given up on men. I had just gotten out of an abusive relationship and I didn't trust men. Derrick is a good man! He is faithful, kind respectful and a good father to his son. Hell, he sure is a better father than I had growing up. My father only came around on the first of the month for about a week and my mother was happy. Later, in life I knew he was coming by to fuck my mother and pretend that he wanted her because she got her welfare check during that time. He used the money that my mother gave him to take care of his other women while we were barely getting by. My mother Eileen loved his dirty drawers, and to this day we can't say anything bad about him.

Growing up, I either saw men that were abusive to women, pimped, got them strung out on drugs or just used them. Derrick was a breath of fresh air because he was different.

I worked my way up from the mail room to an account executive at a major ad agency. I kept attracting bums and hood boys that still lived at home with their mother. I was with my last boyfriend, Trent for four years and in the beginning, he was a great guy. I came home early from work one day and caught him having sex with a bitch in my bed. I mean this muthafucka was hitting this hood bitch raw. Did he not know that he should be protecting not only himself but protect me and his unborn child?

I cleared my throat to let him know that I was there. He turned, looked at me and smiled, but never stopped. I left the house crying and upset and that was the first time that I bumped into Derrick. He helped to calm me down over tea and I thanked him for his assistance but thought nothing more of it. When I returned home later that night Trent was sitting in the living room of the house that I paid all the bills waiting for me. He was upset with me because I came home early.

"Diane, what the hell are you doing coming home early and not telling me?"

I looked at him dumbfounded because I was confused on why I had to tell him that I am coming to my house where I pay all the bills, early. Because I didn't answer him and I was still standing there stuck on stupid, he slapped me.

"Bitch answer me when I'm speaking to you! What the fuck you come home early for? Now you got my bitch upset with me because you interrupted our groove."

"What you mean your girl, you are my live-in boyfriend. She is your hoe and I am your girl."

"Lies you tell! Look Diane everything between us is good because you take care of a nigga and she doesn't want to live with a man that doesn't have his shit together. She knows that you are my roommate only, but you had to fuck that up for me."

"Roommate? Really is that what you tell people that I am your roommate/ Get the fuck out of my house!"

"Your house! Bitch get the fuck away from me before I beat your ass."

"Beat who ass! Trent I am pregnant, and this is how you do me!"

"Pregnant by who?"

"You're the only one I have been with and you know that."

"Diane if you don't get your lying ass out of my house, I swear I will beat the fuck out of you."

"I'm not going anywhere Trent, you need to leave."

"You playing with me Diane and I don't have time for this shit."

As I try to walk past him to go to the room, he grabbed me and tried to push me out the door. I started to fight back. Trent said, "Oh is that what you want, you want to fight." The next thing I felt was his fist crashing into my face. My vision went blurry. That night Trent beat me until I blacked out. When I finally opened my eyes, I was lying in a puddle of blood on the living room floor. My eyes were swollen shut and several of my teeth were lying next to me. I was finally able to get off the floor and go take a shower. When I went to lie in the bed Trent stirred. I didn't want to wake him because I didn't know what he would do next. This is not the first time that he has beaten me like this, and it wouldn't be the last, unless I leave him.

As I lay there Trent turns over and wraps his arms around me and says that he is sorry. "Diane you know you make me crazy. You need to watch your smart mouth. You make me do these things to you."

I never said anything because I didn't want him to hear the fear in my voice or the fact that I was crying.

I slid closer to the edge of the bed just for some space, but he followed me. Trent began to rub on my body, but I moved his hand. He says, "either you're going to give it to me, or I am going to take it. Either way we fucking tonight."

"Trent please my body is hurting, and I can't. I believe you have made me miscarry another baby."

"I don't give a fuck about your body hurting, you will take care of my needs and we won't have a conversation about it."

"Trent I can't!"

The next thing I know is that Trent's hand is around my throat and his other hand is ripping my gown off me. I can only lay there and cry because I am too weak to fight. Trent raped me twice that night. Not only did I lose my baby, I lost all respect for men.

I finally got the nerve to leave one night that week. I had to leave in the middle of the night so he wouldn't beat me again. This is the night I bumped into Derrick again. I had nowhere to go and only forty dollars in my pocket. Derrick saw the bruises that were healing on my face and he offered to help. He got me a room for two weeks until I got my next check. After that night we became inseparable.

CHAPTER 7

Today I start my new journey with getting healthy. I looked through each cabinet and threw away anything that was not healthy. I walked into the gym and it felt like I was walking into a foreign land. I can't do this and as I turned to run out, I bumped into a man that looked like he was dropped from heaven.

"Hold up pretty lady, what's the hurry"

"I'm sorry I wasn't looking. This is my first time at the gym in over ten years and I feel a little intimidated."

"Well don't let it intimidate you. The people here won't bite"

He laughed and of course he had beautiful teeth. Lawd, I am standing in the entry of this gym and this man is making me moist. Ok, I guess I will stick around and do at least one work out. In the back of my head I am thinking I should have started by just walking around the neighborhood. But I'm here now and I might as well workout.

"By the way, I'm Levi."

"Hi Levi, I'm Marie."

"Marie it is definitely my pleasure to meet you and I hope to see you around."

"Well I will be around Levi. Thanks for encouraging me to stay."

I walk over to the front desk to sign up for a membership and get a personal trainer. When Regina and Miracle get here, we'll start our first workout with the personal trainer. I'm not sure if I will be able to concentrate with this fine man training me. I feel like a dog in heat right now and I am ready to pounce.

Mr. Fine is putting a whooping on all of us today and I am ready to cuss his ass out. As we finish our work out and make plans to meet up later for dinner and drinks I bumped into Levi.

"Great workout Marie, when will you be back?"

"Why, I'll be here the next time you're here."

"Well I guess I'll be seeing you tomorrow."

"That soon?"

"HaHaHa, yes that soon. I am here at the gym every day."

"That's a bit much don't you think? You're here at the gym every day? I think you look fine just like you are."

"Thanks for the compliment Marie, but yes there is a need for me to be here every day that the gym is open. Would you like to go over to the smoothie bar and have a drink before you leave?"

"Unfortunately, I can't join you today but maybe another time, I have to go home and get ready."

"I will hold you to that Marie."

This man has me standing is blushing like a teenage school girl. Damn there is that moistness again.

Later that day I fixed myself up and went out to dinner with the girls and guess who we bumped into. If you guessed Derrick, then you guessed correctly. He was sitting in a corner booth with a young woman that I knew was not Diane. I made sure to walk past his table so he could see what he had lost. Derrick looked up when I walked past and almost choked on his drink. I wish I had a man on my arm tonight so I can really watch the bastard choke. Regina, Miracle and I enjoyed our night as we drank and danced the night away.

I really enjoyed myself tonight; I haven't had fun like this since my college days. It is now three o'clock in the morning and I am just getting home, and this asshole is sitting out in my driveway waiting for me.

"Derrick what the hell do you want? Don't you have to be up early in the morning to take your little date to daycare?"

"I'll ignore that comment Marie. What the hell were you doing out in public dressed like that and why the fuck did you cut your hair?"

"Derrick you are not my husband anymore and you have no rights to question me, now what the hell do you want this time of morning?"

"Marie, I don't know who you are anymore, but you need to calm the hell down and get your shit together. Can you also explain why you changed the locks on my damn house?"

"Your house? This is no longer your house. You forfeited your rights to this house when you left me for Diane."

"I never left you for Diane you pushed me to her with all of your bullshit and self-pity."

"So now you're saying that I was pitiful as a wife. Fuck you!"

"Watch your mouth Marie that is not how a lady is supposed to speak."

"Derrick you no longer have the right to tell me anything, again you are no longer my husband."

"Bitch if you say that shit one more time, I swear I will beat your ass!"

"Oh, so there it is, you are truly your father's child."

"Marie why are you making me act this way, you are still my wife until I sign them damn divorce papers."
"Well sign the damn papers then Derrick and let me out of this miserable marriage."

"I refuse to let you go! Marie you and I can get through this just don't leave me."

"Derrick it is done, you left me a long time ago. You were physically there but your mind was always somewhere else. No matter what I did for you it was never good enough. I'm happy now and I just want to be free from you."

"What, you want to be free from me so you can be with someone else? Is this what it's about?"

"It's not about me being with someone else, it's about me loving myself more that I love anyone else. Now don't fool yourself to think that I will be alone for the rest of my life because I won't. I will find me a man that will treat me better than you have ever treated me."

"No one can treat you better than me, I gave you everything. You're the only women I have ever wanted to have my last name."

"You can have your last name! That name has only brought me misery and pain. Anyone that I meet will treat me better than you. Now please leave my house. I'm tired and I have an early day tomorrow."

"I'm leaving but this is not the end of us!"

When I finally got to sleep, I tossed and turned thinking about my life. I wasn't sure if I was making the right decision because Derrick was the only man that I had ever been with. I'm forty years old. Who the hell will want to be with me?

This morning I tried yoga for the first time, and I felt great. As I am leaving my class; guess who I bumped into, Levi.

"Hi Levi!"

"Hey Marie, how was your workout today?"

"It was good; I tried a yoga class today."

"That's wonderful! How did you like it?"

"It was different, but I will definitely be back for another class."

"Cool, you know that offer for the smoothie bar still stands just let me know when you want to go."

As I stand here listening to him talk, in my mind I am saying 'I will go anywhere you want me to go, if you keep looking this fine.'

"Maybe next time Levi; it was good seeing you again."

"The pleasure was all mine Marie."

Every time I see this man, he leaves me blushing and moist, but I am not ready to be with anyone, I'm still working on me.

When I got home, I showered then sat down with a warm cup of tea pondering what I want to do with my life. I have not worked since the beginning of my marriage. As I jot down a few ideas my door bell rings and it is Derrick. I have to pray for strength to deal with his bullshit! I will not let him bring me down today.

"What do you want Derrick, I'm busy!"

"Is that how you greet your husband Marie"

"Husband? Is that what you call yourself Derrick? I believe that you are currently playing house with another woman while you are still collecting toys."

"Marie I am only there because I have nowhere else to go. You put me out remember?"

"I never put you out, you left because you couldn't see the value in our relationship. You had to have multiple women because I just wasn't enough for you. So, what the hell do you want Derrick?"

"Marie things were not working in our marriage and you fail to see what you have done to dissolve this relationship."

"Derrick I'm not be going into this with you today, again what the hell do you want?"

"I was just coming by to check on you and make sure everything is alright. Is there anything that you need; anything that needs to be done around the house? I am just trying to be the husband that I am supposed to be, so you can see that all is not lost with us."

"There is nothing that I want or need from you. Thanks for checking on me but you don't have to ever check again. I'm fine."

"Marie you are talking like this is the final curtain call for our marriage. For me we are not over, I pray for you every night that you remember the good times. I've given you time to cool off now you're just being stupid. Remember that you are nothing without me!"

"Just watch how much of a nothing I will be without you Derrick, now get out!"

Once Derrick left the house, I was able to concentrate on my plans for life. I said a quick prayer then pulled out my laptop to start my job search. I applied for a couple jobs then got up and got dressed to meet the girls for lunch.

Regina and Miracle were already sitting at the table waiting for me when I reached the restaurant.

"Ladies tonight is a shots type of night and drinks are on me."

In unison they say, "Bitch that sounds like a plan"

I proceed to tell them about my yoga class and of course my earlier conversation with Derrick. They don't want to hear anything about Derrick but asked about Levi and of course that silly little grin is on my face.

"Oh Regina, I think she likes him"

"I think you are correct Miracle"

We all laugh loudly until we hear a deep male voice behind us that asked, "What are you beautiful ladies so cheerful about?"

I'd recognize that voice anywhere! I turn around to see Levi standing there with two other guys that I recognized from the gym, he introduces as Romeo and Trent. They were equally as handsome, but Levi had all my attention.

"Oh, it was nothing Levi. I was just explaining my experience in the yoga class this morning."

"Do you ladies mind if we join you at your table? It will be another thirty minutes before we can be seated."

Before I could say anything, Regina and Miracle both said "yes" in unison. As the guys sat down, I gave an evil look to the girls and of course they ignored me. Although the drinks had been flowing the entire night; when the food arrived, Levi took the time to pray over the food. I was very impressed with him. We all enjoyed a nice dinner and conversation. I found out that Levi was from the south side of

Chicago and a business man. The other guys were from Miami. They were frat brothers back in college and have remained close. Romeo was a banker and he was single with no kids. He had his eyes on Regina all night. Trent was a doctor. He was single with no children also. By looking at him you can tell that he had a hard life but had made something of himself. He and Miracle hit it off. After five hours of drinking and getting to know each other we ended our night as the guys walked us out and bided us a goodnight. They were such gentlemen that they waited until we drove off.

CHAPTER 8

"Fellas' that's the woman I have been telling you about, it was a good thing bumping into her outside of the gym. When she's at the gym she seems so guarded but tonight I saw a different side of her. She is not only beautiful on the outside, but I can tell that she has a beautiful soul. I just know that she is the woman that I have been praying for."

Romeo just stares at me as if I have lost my mind and says "Are you sure you want to be with someone right now? Look at all of the shit that Lydia put you through two years ago."

"Look Romeo I am over Lydia and everything to do with her. I think it is time for me to move on and be with a woman. A woman that will allow me to treat her like a queen, not take advantage of me or disrespect me. I believe Marie is that woman. There is something about her that says she needs a man like me in her life. A man that will be her king!"

"But are you ready to be somebody's King? Trent please talk to yo boy."

"Levi, Romeo does have a point. I don't want you to get with a good woman and turn them sour like I did Diane."

"Well this woman is nothing like Diane and I am not you. You have done some messed up things in your life and I am just happy that you got your anger and drinking under control. For a long time, we didn't know the man that you had become. Now that everything is going good in your life it's time for you to find you a good woman also. Romeo that goes for you also!"

"Levi it's going to take a good woman to make me change and I am currently not looking. I'm focusing on my job and this company that we are building:

"Trent you might have found that good woman tonight"

"Who?"

"Come on Trent, I saw how you were looking at Miracle."

"Nawl man; that was your boy Romeo over there drooling all over Regina."

"Who, me?"

"Levi and Trent, you are trying to play me. I am a sworn bachelor for life! I will never be tied down to one woman. I tried that before and I couldn't be faithful remember? Levi, you are the only one that likes to be with one woman."

"Well Romeo you would be wrong. There are a few men in this world that like to be with only one woman. Trent was a player back in the day, but he will settle down as soon as he finds the right woman."

"Levi I can speak for myself. Romeo, I have gotten my life together and I have repented for everything that I have done wrong. I am truly ready to settle down and have children."

"Who the fuck are you and what have you done with my friend."

We are the same guys that you have been around since college, we have just grown into manhood and you are still acting like a little boy.

"Ok, don't get your ass whooped out here in these streets Levi."

Romeo you tried that before and ended up with a broken nose you want another one?

"Man fuck you, I let you get the best of me"

Trent stands there laughing at the foolery going on between Levi and Romeo. You guys need to stop bullshitting' before someone gets hurt out here, Romeo!

Goodnight fellas! I have an early day at the gym in the morning; Marie will be there for class.

They both laugh and say in unison "This muthafucka has become a stalker."

I am far from a stalker I just have a better day when I see her. I haven't felt like this in a long time about a woman. Marie has me intrigued.

You guys have a goodnight and get home safe.

When I got home, I couldn't get Marie off of my mind. I wanted to know if she had gotten home safely. A sat around the house contemplating my next move as I had my night cap; I think I should call her. If I call her, she might be upset and try to figure out how I got her number. That really doesn't matter. I just want to hear her voice. Fuck it, I'm calling!

The phone rang several times before she picked up. Shit I didn't bother to check the clock before I called. She sounded groggy when she answered. Dammit I woke her up.

CHAPTER 9

It's midnight and my phone is ringing, who the fuck is calling me this time of morning. It better not be, Derrick's ass or he will be sorry. For the past couple of weeks, he has been calling me every night. Then I hear a deep sexy male voice and think he must have the wrong number until he says, "Hello Marie".

Hello!

"This is Levi"

"Levi? How did you get my number?"

"I got it from your paperwork at the gym."

"I didn't know they could share my personal information with just anybody."

"The owner is a personal friend of mine and he knows that I am feeling you and he did me a solid."

"A solid? What do you mean by that?"

"I'm sorry about my use of slang but a solid is a favor. As I said I know him personally and he wouldn't normally do this but after hours of begging he finally caved."

"Oh, why would you beg for my number?"

"Marie you are a beautiful woman why I wouldn't want your number."

"Ok, I guess!"

"The problem is that you don't see your own beauty."

"I see my beauty I just don't see it the way that you do."

"We will remedy that! I just wanted to make sure you made it home safely. I also want to say that it was good bumping into you and your friends, and I would like to do it again."

"Look Levi I am married, well technically I am married"

"Oh, I'm sorry I didn't know, I won't bother you again. Have a good night Marie.
You do the same Levi."

After I hung up the phone with Levi I laid there thinking about Levi. This man was fine, but he was too good to be true. It was something about him that had to be wrong. So far everything about this man was good and I wanted him, but I still had to finish this mess with Derrick before I started anything new.

That night I tossed and turned thinking about all the stuff that Derrick put me through and if there was truly a possibility with Levi. That morning when I got up I got on my knees and prayed to God. "Father I come to You right now asking You for strength and healing. I know that You haven't heard from me in a while. but I need Your help right now. For me to move on with my life, I need You to heal my heart and heal my mind. Take away all of this hurt and pain that I have allowed myself to feel. Guide my footsteps and allow me to walk in the purpose that You have set out for me. Guide me O' Lord and have Your way in my life. I need You more now than I have ever needed You before. I have survived off the prayers of my mother and grandmother but today I come to You as humble as I know how. Lord

I need You to restore joy and restore my faith. Continue to watch over me as You have my entire life. Continue to wrap Your loving arms around me. And Lord I know Your Word says that you take care of fools and babies, so Lord please watch over Derrick. Work on him Lord so that he can be a better father to his children and a better man for whatever woman he chooses to be with. Forgive him for his sins. I also ask that You forgive me for any wrongs that I have ever done. This, I ask in Your Name. Amen."

As I finish my prayer, I allow the tears to flow. I have never felt like this. I feel a relief in my body, in my heart and in my mind. I don't know why I ever walked away from my faith and all that I believed, just to please a man. It's a good thing that I know that God will never forsake me. After today my life will be different because I will have control and I will walk in my ordained purpose. I feel like a weight has been lifted off my shoulder and I know I will be ok!

I feel like a new woman!

This morning I am scheduled for a Zumba class. When I got to the gym Levi was nowhere to be found. For some reason it saddens me to think that I have run him off. I looked forward to seeing him whenever I came to the gym.

I finished my class and I am exhausted. On my way out I stop by the juice bar for a strawberry banana smoothie and there I finally bumped into Levi.

"Hi Levi"

"Hi Marie!"

"Why do you look like you have lost your best friend?"

"I lost the woman of my dreams so it's like I lost my best friend."

"Levi, let's have dinner tonight and we can talk."

"Are you sure your husband will allow you to go out on a date with me."

"That is what we need to talk about. I'll see you tonight, is seven o'clock a good time for you."

"Seven o'clock is perfect. Would you like me to pick you up?"

"Thanks for the offer but I'll meet you at the restaurant. Let's exchange numbers and I'll call you with the details later today."

That afternoon I called Levi and asked if he would mind meeting me at the local lounge for dinner and dancing. He was ok with that, now I had to call my girls to assist me with my outfit. I have picked out several, but I don't really know which one is best. It has been a very long time since I have dressed for a date. Let alone have a man that was interested in me. I won't read too much into this night because Levi could truly be a good friend.

Once Regina and Miracle arrived, I had everything laid out for them on my bed. It looked like a hurricane had hit my room because I had shoes and clothes everywhere. I was a nervous wreck! Miracle was the first to come in my room.

"Girl what the hell was you thinking with some of these outfits? You are going to club not to church?"

"Shut up, Miracle I haven't done this in a while, and I don't want to be too slutty"
.
"Slutty is the only way to go with a man like Levi."

"I can tell that he is a great catch, but I don't want him to think that I am easy."

"Marie you haven't gotten any in a while."

"HaHaHa you surely have jokes, Regina please come get this girl."

"Well Marie I agree with Miracle you do need to get laid."

"You too! Regina."

"This is not about me this is about you and your date; now let us help you get ready."

I looked at myself in the mirror after getting dressed and damn I looked good. Regina had laid my hair. Miracle had picked out this little black sexy number. We all agreed that I should wear the black and gold Michael Kors heels that I had purchased on one of our recent shopping trips. I was very proud in the way that I looked. I had changed my mind after all and called Levi to pick me up for our date. I wanted to be able to drink and enjoy our night together.

Levi picked me up around seven o'clock. When he got to the door, he had two dozen cream and white tulips with lilies. It had been a very long time since someone bought me flowers. He made sure all my doors and windows were locked before leaving the house. So far, I was very impressed with him.

On our way over to the club we listened to soft jazz playing while we conversed about the latest topics that were going on in the world. We also talked about my work search and he agreed to help me by putting me in contact with a couple of headhunters he knew.

As we pulled up to the club it was crowded of course. I started having second thoughts about being here. I have not stepped foot into a club since college. We are here now, and this was my idea. We were walked to our table as soon as we walked into the club. A nice-looking young man came and greeted Levi at the table. I later found out that the club was owned by his brother Arnold.

I was very pleased with the ambience and the service so far. The club was called Lady Bella. The place was decorated in white and purple with crystal chandeliers. The flower arrangements on each table had cream and white roses, tulips and lilies with lavender. I later found out that it was named after their mother Bella. Everything about the club had been decorated to bring back a certain memory of her. It was a very cozy atmosphere with dim lighting. Each night there was a local jazz band that came out and played.

We ordered our drinks. I had a Tropical Martini and he had a Hennessey on the rocks. I felt very giddy being that I have not been on a date in years.

Derrick never took me out unless it was for my birthday and occasionally for an anniversary dinner.

I can tell that Levi was very different. He was a breath of fresh air. Every time this man looked at me or touched me, I got goose bumps then I would feel wetness in between my legs. Not even Derrick has ever made me feel that way. I just might have to rethink this thing with Levi because this attraction that I have with him is starting to scare the hell out of me.

CHAPTER 10

Here I am sitting here having a nice evening with Diane and I spot Marie coming in here with another man. This is not the Marie that I know. My wife would never be out this late. She would never dress like that. I hope she remembers that she is a married woman. She hasn't dressed like that for me in a very long time.

"Honey is there something wrong? I thought you were enjoying your evening with me?"

"Diane everything is fine, why do you ask?"

"Derrick you seem so distracted and you looking over there at that table. Do you know that woman?"

"Will you shut the hell up Diane and stop asking me questions! Just be happy that I am out with you tonight."

"Well you have been very distant lately and I can't understand why. I do everything that you ask me to do. I cook, clean, and make sure our son is well cared for. You wanted another woman in our bed and I even allowed you to do that."

"Allowed? Bitch, you are gonna always do what the hell I want you to do or find yourself back on the street looking for that doggish ass nigga that use to beat your ass!"

"I'm not sure what you have going on in your life but I'm tired of you threatening me!"

"Baby it's not a threat' I just always want you to remember that I made you into the woman you are today."

"You didn't make me Derrick!"

"Let's go Diane you have ruined my night. It's time that I drop you off at home".

"What do you mean drop me off at home?'

"Just what the fuck I said!"

"So where are you going this late at night?"

"Mind your damn business woman, I have told you before to never question me. As long as I take care of you and the house, I don't answer questions. I am the man in this relationship not you!"

"Fuck you Derrick; I am so tired of your bullshit!'

"You can dry up those crocodile tears. We were having a good evening, but you had to ruin things with that mouth of yours."

As we rode to the house in silence, I was getting more pissed that Marie had the nerve to be out on what looks like at date. She is going around acting as if she doesn't have a husband. When she gets home, I will be there waiting for her ass. She has some explaining to do.

We finally made it home and I made sure that Diane made it in the house safe. I sat with her for a moment but all she did was complain about me leaving the house again this late in the evening. I decided to stay home for about thirty minutes to let her calm down. As we are sitting here, I feel Diane hands in my pants. She was gonna try to do everything in her power to make me stay.

"Diane, I am not having sex with you. I just told you that I was going out tonight." She just dropped to her knees as if she didn't hear anything, I was saying to her. Once she had me in her mouth, I was not going to make her stop. This is one of the many reasons that I am with her. Diane is a very nasty girl when it comes to bedroom activities. She allows me to do anything and everything that I want to her.

Oh, she was so beautiful on her knees with my dick in her mouth. While she was taking all ten inches of my thick dick down her throat she was playing with her pussy. I was so gone that I never seen her pull the dildo out. She fucked herself while I gagged her with my dick. I was able to get all of me down her throat as I saw the tears in her eyes, but she would not pull it out. Diane was a good bitch. I fucked her throat with no mercy like it was her pussy. It felt like I was trying to fuck her voice away. I pulled her up off the floor and bent her over. She still had the dildo in her pussy, so I put my dick on her asshole and entered. As my entire dick entered her ass, she screamed loud and began to cry but I didn't stop. I had no mercy on her. I was mad and I was taking all my anger out on her. If she had just let me leave, she would not have been in this situation right now. I fucked her with no mercy for a good thirty minutes. Once I pulled out, I stuck my dick back down her throat and came.

I went to shower to get her smell off me. I left her lying on the living room floor when I left the house. I can tell that she was crying but I really didn't care. I had to get my wife back.

I sat outside Marie's house for hours waiting for her to return home. While I was there, I thought about the woman that I took for granted. She was the true essence of a woman. Marie cooked, cleaned and did everything that she was taught to do by her mother as a wife. She not only prayed for me, but she prayed with me. She was my covering in this crazy world that I lived in. I know that I took her for granted but I never thought she would leave me. There has to be a way that I can convince her to stay with me.

Over a year ago Marie wrote me a letter because she said I don't listen when she speaks. I have read that letter daily for the past month since she sent me divorce papers. As I sit here waiting for her, I am reminiscing on the words that she pours out in the letter.

Dear Derrick,

I really don't know where to go from here. You have done so much in this marriage to hurt me. I don't know how to repair this relationship. I am completely torn inside and every day I am trying to be whole again. The love I have for you has never faded and I still see myself with you in the future. I want the life with you that I pictured in the beginning stages of our relationship. I forgave you for the relationship and child that you had with Regina but yet you still continue to ruin our union. In the beginning it was me and you only but somewhere down the line you lost the sense of who you are. Instead of growing together you grew apart from seeking things and people outside of our marriage. I thought life with you was going to be different but for our own selfish reasons we just can't seem to make things work. These relationships that you have with all these other women are something that I can't handle.

I pray for you every day that you only have eyes for me, but I don't ever see that happening. I now know that you are searching for something that you still have not found. When we first got together everything was fine, but when I gained weight and couldn't give you a baby; things became different. Yes, you were still attracted to me sexually, but I saw the way you would look at other women. I knew *what my body looked like and you made me become ashamed of myself more than I already was.*

I hate the woman that I have become being in this marriage. I have become bitter, insecure, untrustworthy, fragile, lonely and I feel desperate at times. You have broken me down to my core and I don't know how to repair myself.

I want to be happy and want a man to love me and only me. I don't want a man that I have to share with another woman. I want to be loved and feel loved by you. I want the type of confidence that when we go out, I feel that no other female in the room is better than me. No female can take my husband from me. I don't feel that way ever. I want confidence in my marriage. Confidence to know that my husband loves me and only me!! When we first got together there was nothing in the world that would show me that anyone else could have my husband.

Life for us has not been great and I want them to get better. Our life can be better we have just got to put in the work to make it better. If we truly want this marriage to work, we should be praying for and with each other, we should be in our bible together. There are so many things that we should be doing to make our relationship better, but you spend so much time hiding things, sneaking and lying and it has got to stop.

When you look at me, I see the disappointment and lack of respect for me in your eyes and I don't know how to get it back. We are both hurting, and we need to work on this together. If you truly want this marriage to work, we must put our differences to the side and learn to love each other again. I want to feel secure with you again! I want my family!

I just want my friend, my husband, my lover and my confidant back! I love you no matter if you stay with me or not! I want you to be happy!

As the tears fall down my face, I now know that it took for me to see Marie with another man to understand her need. Now don't get me wrong I want her to be happy, but only with me. Tomorrow I am moving out of the house with Diane and back with my wife. I will do everything in my power to get the love of my life back.

After sitting here for hours Marie finally came home.

CHAPTER 11

After enjoying my night out with Levi, I come home only to see Derrick's car sitting in my driveway. I have had a wonderful night and I don't feel like his drama.

"Baby it looks like you have company"

"It's nobody; would you like to come in for a nightcap?"

"Sure!"

As we are approaching Derrick jumps out of his car screaming like the idiot he is.

"Who the fuck is this clown?"

"Look Derrick just go home to your little girlfriend and leave me alone!"

"I am home, what the fuck are you talking about. This is my motherfucking house.
I pay all the bills up in this bitch!"

"Can you please take your lying cheating ass back to one of your many sluts? What,' one of them put you out so you are now back on my doorstep? If that is the case, then you must find somewhere else to go because you can't stay here."

"Look bitch I've told you about your smart-ass mouth! This is my house and if I want to be here, I will be here. There is nothing you can do about."
"I am not sure who you are, but I will not stand here any longer and allow you to disrespect Marie any further."

"Man fuck you! This is my wife and I can speak to her anyway I damn well feel!'

"Well if you were her husband, she wouldn't be out on a date with me!"

"You must really want your ass beat out here!'

"Both of you stop!" I screamed so loud and all the commotion going on is starting to wake up my neighbors. "Derrick you go home please! Just sign the damn papers and allow me to be free. You have already proven to me that you don't want me, just go and let me be happy!" I am now crying hysterically, and Levi has come by my side to console me. I can see the anger in Derrick's eyes but there is nothing that he can do about it.

Before Derrick left, he turned and said "Marie I love you and I really want to make our marriage work. I know that I have done you wrong, but I still love you and I can make it work with you. I will let everyone that I am dealing with go because you are all that I want."

Hearing him say the words that I have been waiting so long made me want to call him back, but I couldn't. I knew that he would never change for me. Derrick needs to make changes in his life to make himself better and he is not ready to do that.

Levi walked me in the house. We sat on the couch and he held me until I had depleted myself of tears. At that moment I knew that he was the man that God had sent in my life. I wasn't sure if he was sent to be a friend or to be my man. All I know is that right now, at this very moment he was the shoulder I needed to cry on.

"Thank you for staying here with me. I'm sorry that you had to hear all the drama that's currently happening in my life. Right now, I'm emotionally torn, and I am seeking direction and purpose for my life. I appreciate the attention that you are showing me. You being here is just what the doctor ordered."

We both stood, and I looked into Levi's eyes and all I see is understanding. I walked him to the door and we just stood there. I felt comfortable in his presence. There was something about him that made me feel protected. At the door he said "Just remember in life you do what makes you happy. Don't live your life trying to make everyone around you happy. Someone who really loves you can see the person that you are. A beautiful person can bring things into your life that all the money in the world couldn't obtain. He then kissed me on my forehead and left."

I went to bed and cried but I was happy that God had placed Levi in my life. I woke up the next morning to the sound of my doorbell ringing. I wonder who the hell was at my door this early without calling first? When I got to the door it was a flower delivery. I got excited until I saw that the card was from Derrick. I opened the card and it said:

Dear Wife,

I want you to know that I apologize for all the wrong that I have done in our marriage. I love you more than anything in this world. I can't imagine my life without you. I promise to do right this time. We can go to counseling like you wanted to. I will go to church with you every Sunday. Whatever you are requiring of me I will do it. I just want my wife back. I am miserable without you. Please let me come home.

Love: Your Husband

I tossed the flowers in the trash and dressed and got myself ready for the gym. Before I got in the shower, I checked my voicemail and there was a lady that called about a job. I made a note to contact the office once they opened.

Things were finally falling in place for me and I was not going to let Derrick ruin it!

CHAPTER 12

After I got home last night I was worried about Marie. I could see the hurt in her eyes when she looked at her husband. I never want to see a woman hurting the way she was. I know that we were placed in each other lives for a reason. I have finally picked the pieces of my life up after almost losing every. The most important thing that I did loose was my wife. Just the thought of Bridgett makes me smile.

It's been five years since she died. On her way home from work she was hit by a drunk driver. The paramedics found her emergency contact card that stated to call Trent. She knew that I would be a wreck and couldn't handle it. He called and asked me to meet him at Saint Mary's hospital. Once I got there my world came crashing down.

Trent was waiting in front of the hospital for me. As he was speaking, I saw his lips moving but I couldn't really hear what was being said due to my state of shock.

"Levi, its Bridgett, she was in a horrible accident on her way home from work. They are working on her now, but it doesn't look good."

"What do you mean it doesn't look good?"

"Levi we just need to pray for her right now."

As the tears are streaming down my face I began to pray.

"Father God please don't take my wife. She is my one true love that You designed just for me. I can't live my life without her. You told me that if I was faithful to Your Word that You would supply my needs. I need Bridgett in my life God. Please hear my cry."

"Levi the doctor is here, he needs to speak with you."

Walking towards the doctor was the hardest walk of my life. My steps felt heavy. I was physically there, but mentally I was not prepared for what he had to say. When he spoke, I felt life leaving my body.

"Mr. Brown, I am sorry to inform you that your wife and child did not survive the accident. We have tried all that we could to save both."

I sat there, void of life trying to comprehend what he was saying. "Child, what child?" Oh, thank God they have the wrong woman. Bridgett wasn't pregnant.

"Doctor Lee, I'm sorry but my wife wasn't pregnant."

"Mr. Brown she was identified already by your friend Mr. Lee."

"I need to see her for myself to make sure that it is her."

"Ok."

As we walked to the emergency operating room, I couldn't bring myself to go in. Trent placed a reassuring hand on my back, and we walked into the room together. When I saw my beautiful wife lying on that table, I lost it. I had never cried in front of other people like that in my life. I cried for the loss of my wife and the unborn child that I never knew she was caring.

Trent handled all the arrangements for the funeral. I tried to be strong for her family, but I just couldn't take seeing her lying there. I got up and walked out of the church. I drove with no destination in sight, but I just had to get away from the hurt and pain I was feeling.

It was five months before I spoke to anyone. When I returned home my brothers had removed all of Bridgette's things from the house. My master bedroom was now my office. The guest bedroom was now my master bedroom. I was very appreciative for all that they had done. I didn't know what I was going to do with the house once I returned home. My brothers made sure I was ok.

After my time away I quit my job as a banker and opened my gym. I had spent too much time in the corporate world and had forgot about all the things that mattered. Bridgette spent many days and nights begging for me to come home early from work. She wanted me to spend more time with her, but I had failed her. Now that she's, gone I will use my life to help others renew themselves. Owning the gym will allow me to be a positive light in the community and help those around me get physically healthy.

The gym became my life!

The day I met Marie coming through my doors I knew that she was hurting on the inside. Her soul was calling to my soul. I felt a strong connection to her, and I knew that she would be in my life for a long time. I am attracted to her in every way a man can be to a woman. Right now, she needs a friend and I will be that. If it is God's plan for us to be together it will happen when it's time.

CHAPTER 13

I can't believe that Derrick treated me like I was a whore. He has never treated me like that before. I am not sure what changed when we were at dinner to make him so upset. Lately he has been very distant with me and I just want to make things work for us. We are a family, but he was still legally married to Marie. Every time I ask why he has not gotten a divorce he would get upset and say that Marie would not sign the papers. I am not sure why she won't sign the papers he is not with her. There must be more to the story. I just don't understand why she is holding on to a man that doesn't want her.

I know I deserve better. Every man that I have had in my life has treated me like shit. I give my all to these men but in return they give me their ass to kiss. Last night Derrick went from loving me to hurting me. I try to be the woman to him that he wants me to be. The woman that Marie could never be for him!

My mother has always told me that I would be good for nothing but lying on my back. She said that no man would ever love me because I took the love of her life away from her. You see my mother was sat to marry her high school sweetheart, but she was raped by one of his teammates. I was conceived from that rape. Her mother, my grandmother did not believe in abortions, so she was forced to have me. When her fiancé found out that she was pregnant he left her for cheating on him. He was told by his teammate that she gave it to him willingly. Because he believed him, he refused to marry my mother. On that very date my mother began her hate for me.

After I was born my grandmother took care of me because my mother wouldn't touch me. My mother only did things for me financially. Eventually she met a man that would later become her pimp. He introduced her to drugs and the fast life. She sold her body for drugs and money. Once he began taking her money, she was no longer able to support me. I was left to fend for myself, my grandmother refused to help. When I was younger, I didn't know that my mother was not only taking care of me financially, but she paid my grandmother to do so. When the money ran out so did my grandmothers love. What type of love was that!

As I sit here and think about my life I begin to cry. I have lost myself in all this drama in my life. I thought things were getting better for me. I am a long way from being prostituted at the age of thirteen. Yep you heard me; my mother sold me to the highest bidder for one hundred dollars. At twelve her pimp Johnny began to groom me. My virginity was taken by a fifty-year-old man. He taught me everything that I need to know to please a man. My first lesson was how to properly suck a dick. He kept me in a room and beat me until I could suck his dick without choking or throwing up. My mother was there but she did nothing to help. Once I mastered oral sex he moved to vaginal sex. The smell of his skin was sickening but I had to do it in order to survive.

He made me dance for him while I took my clothes off. Once I was undressed, he laid me on the bed and began to fondle my body. Just feeling his hands on my body made my skin crawl. Mr. Johnny stuck his nasty tongue in my mouth, and I wanted to bite it off, but I know that would be trouble. I just went with the flow of things. He then started kissing me on my neck as his fingers roamed my pussy. His fingers hurt so badly but I could not let him see me cry. Once he started kissing my breast taking each one in his mouth. One at a time he rolled his tongue around my nipples. The sensation from this was doing something strange things to my body. He slowly made his way down to my pussy. I covered my face with my hands. Why was he down there like that? What was he doing? Pee comes from there! It was nasty for him to be down there.

Before I could ask a question, I felt his mouth on me. At first it felt like someone was tickling me. After a while I started to enjoy it. The sensation of what he was doing was making me feel warm throughout my body. He pushed his fingers deep inside me but this time I didn't feel any pain. He kept his face there moving his tongue around my pearl then in and out of my vagina. The feeling was taking over my body and I couldn't control myself. Johnny continued to swirl his tongue around my pearl until it felt like I was peeing on myself. He kept his fingers inside me and just laughed. I screamed and my body went into convulsions, but I didn't know what was going on. Johnny refused to take his fingers out he just put more in me. I kept screaming "Johnny please stop I'm peeing on myself." That just made him laugh even harder.

Once my body calmed down, he got up and just looked at me. Johnny said, "you are one pretty little lady and I am glad that I got the opportunity to have you before any other man could ruin you." When he took his pants off, I just stared because there was no way that that thing was going to fit in me. It was one thing to take his fingers and tongue, but his dick was too big for me. Johnny came to the bed and lay beside me. He kissed me and I could taste myself on him. I scrunched my face up and he laughed and said "get used to it; you'll learn to like it. If you don't like the taste of yourself then no man will."

Johnny put my hand on his dick, and I began to rub on it. He asked if I was ready for him. I knew I wasn't ready, but I knew it was going to happen rather I wanted it to or not. He leaned over me and put the head of his dick at the entrance of my core. He tried to enter but he was too big for me. Johnny had an eight-inch-thick dick trying to penetrate a virgin twelve-year-old. He wasn't being gentle with me either. He pushed and pushed until I felt a tear in my body. I screamed so loud that the neighbors should have heard me. All mama said was shut up that goddamn noise before I beat your ass.

Johnny stuck a dirty towel in my mouth and began to fuck me hard. All he kept saying is "damn girl this pussy is so tight. You are going to make us a lot of money." I cried the entire time. It felt like the sex would never end. When he finally finished my body was bruised, worn and tired. But the worst thing that happed was he had broken my spirit. Every night after that Johnny would come to my room and have sex with me. I eventually started to enjoy it. My mom started to resent me more because I was taking her man. I was offering him something that she couldn't; a sweet tight juicy pussy.

For a year Johnny was my man and it cause a major rift between me and my mom. Because he was with me, she had to go back on the street like the common whore she was. One day when Johnny was gone, she sold me to one of her johns for one hundred dollars and drugs. She told me if I ever come back to her house, she would kill me. I believed everything that she said because she had already brought me close to death before. Her john uncle Curtis as he wanted to be call was a big-time drug dealer. He treated me like I was his wife. I kept his house cleaned, cooked, and entertained his friends. With him was the first time I had been with a woman.

At first, I refused to be with her. He took me into the other room and beat me until I could not open my right eye. He picked me up from the floor and choked me until I started turning red in the face.

With a deadly stare he said "you are going to go in that room and please my girlfriend. Once you are done with her, I have a special treat for you." I got up fixed myself up the best that I could and went in the room and pleased her just as Johnny had taught me to do. I used all the toys and devices that Curtis had laying out for me. She really enjoyed it, but I was disgusted. When I was finished with her, he took me into another room where there were twelve guys lined up to have sex with me. I began to cry but Curtis looked at me and told me to get my ass in the room. I walked in the room and the first guy grabbed me and pushed me down and shoved his dick down my throat. I choked and vomited all over the place. Curtis walked over and slapped me so hard that my other eyed was swollen shut.

Guy number two shoved his dick down my throat. He told me if I vomited on him, he would beat my ass. All the guys started circling around me. I was using my hands and mouth to please these guys. Someone bent me over and started fucking me. I cried the entire time. It took them four hours to get their fill of me. They fucked me in every hole on my body. Tonight, I had my first anal experience. The only reason Johnny never did that was because he thought it was nasty. Well Curtis didn't think so. One of the guys attempted to do it but Curtis said that he would be the one to break me in. I pleaded with him not to do it, but my cries went on death ears.

Curtis came over and spit on my ass then put anal probe up my ass. Once he felt I was ready, he rammed his twelve-inch dick up my ass. This was the worst pain that I had ever felt in my life. I screamed and cried, and he held me down and continued to fuck me with no mercy. My ass was on fire and there was blood everywhere. When he was done with me, he left me lying there for the other guys to do their business. This night I also experienced my first double penetration. These guys used my body. I felt degraded, used and abused. When they were done with me Curtis made me clean up the house before I can go to bed. I sat in a tub of hot water to soothe my aches and pain. There must be a way out of this I just have to figure it out.

I endured the torture from Curtis and any other man that he let abuse my body for several months. I finally got the nerve to run when I was sixteen. That is when I ran into Trent. I thought he would be my saving grace because he treated me so much different than all the other guys. For the first year of our relationship everything was perfect. Once I told him my life story, he started to treat me different. He would beat me and told me that he would treat me like the whore that I was. The problem with him was that I thought that he loved me, but his behavior showed me differently. The love of my life turned into the devil. After Trent, I met Derrick.

Derrick was going through some things in his life with his wife Marie. We used to sit and talk for hours about life. We discussed our future goal. Somewhere down the line we just connected. We became lovers and friends. I knew that he was married but he was going to leave his wife. Derrick was the first guy in my life that taught me to love my body. Sex with him was amazing. He made me feel like I was the only woman in the world. After a year of us dating I found out that I was pregnant with our son. When I told Derrick, it was the happiest that I had ever seen him. I knew of the issues that he and his wife had trying to conceive a child. She couldn't give it to him, but I could.

Since I was pregnant, Derrick moved in with me. I was enjoying our family. There were nights that he would disappear, but he would tell me that he was with Marie discussing their divorce. I know that this doesn't take all night, but I refuse to mess up my happy home. I just let him be. He promised that he would never treat me the way every other guy has, but last night he did. The way that Derrick treated me made me feel like trash again. I lay on that cold floor and cried myself to sleep. When I awakened this morning, I cleaned the house and prepared dinner. I would later go to pick up my son. I would wait for Derrick to come home so I can apologies for upsetting him. I know I caused him to treat me that way.

CHAPTER 14

I have spent the last week playing the nice guy. I don't see why Marie doesn't see that I am a good guy. I have rented a small condo near the house that we share together. She needs to see that we belong with each other. I can't make it knowing that Marie is in the arms of another man. What the hell is she thinking cheating on me?

I know that I am wrong for being upset because of the shit that I have done. All of the women that I have slept with have put a strain on our marriage. For me I wasn't doing anything wrong. My father always told me that I should have as many women as I could handle. My mother always told me to have one woman and love her. She never wanted me to put any woman through the things that my father put her through. I am a little bit of both my parents. I have the kind heart of my mother. I had the lustful eye of my father.

Although I loved Marie, I wanted more than she was willing to give. She was the perfect woman but was afraid to take risk. Marie took care of me and the house like she was taught. She taught me to love and respect others.

It only took me to see her with another man to change me. I am used to doing whatever I want with whoever I want. Being a CEO of a fortune five hundred company allows me to live the life that I always dreamed about. I travel a lot for work and Marie has always accepted that. On many of my trips I would take another woman with me. These women never cared about me being married. They were only concerned of what they got out of the deal. I'd spend a few dollars on them. Show them a good time then dick them down and everything was good. Everyone knew if they saw me out in the street to act like they didn't know me.

People would be surprised of the women that I choose to date. No matter what I always kept me a ghetto hood rat on my team. This type of woman is that nasty bitch that will allow a man to do anything to her. Hell, she will even let his friends hit it for the right price. Keisha was my hoe of choice. She had no respect for herself. Her loyalty was to the dollar.

There was my boss's wife. I could always tell by the way she looked at me that she wanted me. She had never been with a black man before. The first time I had sex with her was at a work convention. She came on the trip with her husband. Her and her husband Dan stayed in a different hotel than I did. This was a working vacation for them. After we finished up at the convention Dan went to his hotel and I went to mine. When I got to my room Melanie was laying on my bed waiting for me. I was startled at first not knowing if this was a set up. I couldn't lose my job over some pussy.

I asked her, "what the hell do you think you are doing?" and "how the hell did you get in here?"

She said, "oh I just told the front desk that I was your secretary and needed to get something out of your room."

"What if your husband comes looking for you?"

"He won't Derrick, I'm sure he is already in the bed."

"Look Melanie' I think you are beautiful, but I am not going to lose my job over some pussy. You need to leave."

As I finished saying that I felt her unzip my pants and began to rub my dick.

"Are you sure you want me to leave?"

By this time, she has my manhood in her mouth, and it feels so damn good. I just stand there and allow her to do what she came to do. I was impressed because this was the first time that a bitch had put my entire dick down their throat. Melanie was a real nasty bitch and I loved it. When she finished sucking my dick she stood and bent over in front of me.

"Fuck me Derrick! I've been waiting for this for a long time now." I pulled a condom from my wallet and gave her what she asked for. I spit on my hand and rubbed it on her pussy then entered her hard and fast. I made sure that every inch of me entered her. Melanie screamed so loud I just knew that someone was going to call security. She turned to me and said "I like that nigga, now fuck me until I see stars. Fuck me until I can't walk straight."

I didn't know if I should be offended that she called me a nigga or not, but I didn't care. That night I gave her what she asked for and I fucked the shit out of her. Every hole of her body was filled with this big black nigga dick. When I finished, I didn't allow her to sleep. I told her to get dressed and get the fuck out. Although I was mad at her I fucked her every night of the convention.

Then there was Theresa. She was this freak from a marketing firm that occasionally worked with our company. We were working late one summer night. Our affair started because the air conditioning unit was broken.

It was hot and steamy in the office; our clothes were wet because of the heat. She pulled her hair out of her usual bun and I was mesmerized. She was

African and Puerto Rican mixed with these beautiful brown almond shaped eyes. I always thought that she was beautiful but never crossed the line. We had a working relationship only until this day. She then unbuttoned her shirt exposing her perky c-cup breast and I immediately wanted to pop one in my mouth. Theresa took a towel out of her purse and began to dab it on her face, neck and chest. My dick instantly became hard. Obviously, she saw this because she looked at me with a sly smile.

I asked what are you smiling for and she said "Because Mr. wants to come out to play. I always knew that you wanted me, but you were scared to make a move on me."

First let's get one thing straight Theresa, "I'm never scared of any woman!"

She just laughed and said, "If you're not scared of me then come over here and eat this pussy."

I sat there contemplating my next move. When I looked up, she had her skirt lifted and she wasn't wearing panties. I got up and locked the door and walk over to her. I asked, "are you sure you want this"? Once I get started, I will be fucking you. Theresa just looked at me and spread her legs. I dropped to my knees and devoured her. I ate her until she couldn't come anymore. Then I bent her over and fucked her. When I finished fucking her, she couldn't walk straight.

She looked up at me from the desk in my office and smiled. She then said, "If I had known you were a beast like that, I would have been fucked you."

Things with us continued for about a year. It worked because I was married and so was, she. This was the perfect match for me until she became pregnant. She soon began to hate me because I made her have an abortion. I mean she couldn't have my baby. How would I explain that to Marie and how would she explain that to her husband? I know I was wrong to be having sex with her without protection but hey the pussy was good.

Things with us ended badly and eventually she stopped coming to my office but sending someone else to take over the account.

Being with all these women I know that I have hurt Marie. I just knew that she would always be there for me just like my mother was for my dad. Not only has the hurt that I have caused her bothered me, but the disappointment that I see in her eyes when she looks at me. I have got to find a way to get her back. Maybe I need counseling for my addiction to sex...

Yeah that's it! I'm addicted to sex!

I must let all these women go. I haven't called Diane in weeks. I have only seen Kami twice. Yes, I am remorseful, but a brother does need to fuck from time to time. After my meeting with Kami tonight I am leaving all these women alone and working on myself.

I'm determined to get the love of my life back!

CHAPTER 15

Marie

Now that I am working, I am spending less time at the gym. For some reason I crave the presence of Levi. Right now, we are nothing more than friends, but he means a lot to me. He is helping me through this difficult time of me, finding me. There have been several nights that I have called him, and he was there for me. No, he doesn't come to my house, but he answers. No matter when I call, he is there to let me cry or talk. He prays for me and with me. I have never had a man that prays for me. I am starting to feel Levi on a different level, but I don't know how he feels about me. Tonight, when I speak with him, I will bring up the topic.

Working has a feeling of accomplishment for me. I let myself go in order to please a man. I now have an investment in my future. I am learning to love the skin that I'm in. Derrick thought that he broke me down, and for a while he did. But I have found my strength. I let him abuse me too long.

I never thought I was an abused woman, but I was. It wasn't physical, so I thought I could work through my marriage woes. I now know and accept that my abuse was mental. The things he said and did was me losing myself and allowing him to control who I was. I did everything that he wanted me to do but it wasn't enough.

I didn't buy my own clothes Derrick did. He was always afraid that another man would look at me and claim his prize as he would say. Hell, if I was a prize to him it must have been one from the Cracker Jack box because that's how he treated me.

I have found me, and I love her!

Tonight, the girls and I are going to dinner to celebrate my new job. It feels good to be celebrated. I went out and got me a cute little black dress for tonight. It shows off all my curves. Although things aren't its best right now my life is great! Life can only get better from here.

Today is my first day working at the advertising agency as an account representative. When I walk into my office wearing my white Vera Wang pantsuit with a multi-colored blouse I found at the local Target store and my Christian Louboutin gold pumps, I feel like a million bucks. I am all nerves inside, but I know I can do this.

I walk into my office and there are two flower deliveries sitting on my desk. I go to read the card of the one holding pure white lilies. It was from Levi and the card reads: "Congratulations! You will do great today. Remember to pray this morning that your steps are ordered. If you need me, I am only a phone call away". I looked up and said 'God thank you for placing this man in my life. I don't know his reason for being here but thank you!"

The other vase was filled with pure white and lavender tulips. It was from the girls. These girls have truly had my back over the years, and I am proud to call them my sisters.

My new boss Stephanie came in and introduced me to the staff. We went over my duties and I was given my student assistant. This job hires students as the assistants in order to give them experience. This working knowledge helps them to better compete in the marketing field once they graduate. My assistant's name was Kami Landry. Kami was a young woman that was in college on a college scholarship. She is from the inner-city and I will be proud to work with her.

She came in and introduced herself to me. She looked familiar but I didn't know where I knew her from. I shook her hand and told her that it was going to be a pleasure getting to know her. Looking over her file was very impressive. She had a 4.0 GPA and was the first in her family to go to college. She had been through some tough times in her life, but she made it out. Reading this made me want to help her even more.

After diving into my work assignments, I heard a knock on the door. It was Kami. She wanted to know if I was going out to lunch. I hadn't realized that time had passed by that fast. I looked at my watch and noticed that it was 1:30pm. I began to grab my things and headed to the door. I stopped at Kami's desk and said, "why don't you come to lunch with me, my treat." She looked at me hesitantly but said what the heck.

We went down to a little café across the street from our building. We sat and talked to get to know one another better. I told her that I was returning to the workforce after a loveless marriage. I was happy to finally be here doing things for myself. If feels good not to have to depend on someone else. She told me about her life growing up in the inner-city. She was twenty and had to help her mother take care of her siblings. Her mother had a way of picking no good men as her children's father. Kami laughed at that, but I could see the hurt in her eyes. She then told me about this guy that she had been seeing. He was an older guy. She wanted more from the relationship, but she felt that he was only using her for sex. My response was if you know you are only being used for sex why do you keep seeing him.

"Well Marie, I think I am falling in love with him."

"A man only using you for sex isn't love!"

"We don't only have sex. He helps me out financially also."

"Then that is prostitution, Kami!"

She got upset grabbed her stuff and walked away from the table. When I got back to the office, she was sitting at her desk working. For the remainder of the day she would not make eye contact with me and only came in my office when it was necessary.

I felt bad and wanted to apologize. I wasn't calling her a prostitute. To each its own. If that is how she gets by that is her life not mine, I truly don't care. When I left the office, Kami was already gone. I left her a note to stop by my desk in the morning.

I rushed home and showered and prepared my clothes for work on tomorrow. I knew this was going to be a long night. We were meeting up at the same restaurant that Levi had taken me. As usual the girls were running late. I was greeted by Levi's brother the owner. He smiled when he saw me and said "Hey Pretty Lady! How are you on this fine evening?" Your friends called and asked me to take care of you until they got here. Unfortunately, I am swamped tonight but my hostess will be taking good care of you. Whatever you need ask her and it's yours. The hostess walked to a back room and when she opened the doors my friends were there. They had secretly set up a private party for me. Levi and his friends were there. My mother-in-law and Miracle's mother even came out tonight. All I could do was cry tears of joy. Today I know that I am truly loved.

We all talked, ate, and laughed. During the evening I kept seeing my mother in law watching me. She eventually pulled me to the side. Her words made me cry because at that moment we connected. She said "Marie know that I will always love you as my daughter no matter what. I am very happy for you.

You had the courage to do what I never could do. I am happy to see the light back in your eyes. Over the years your vision of love became cloudy because you were blinded by what you thought was love. That man over there that I keep seeing looking at you, don't discount him because of what another man has done. I have had conversations with him tonight and he is a different type of man. Levi is a God-fearing man. Accept love again; don't let Derrick make you bitter. I'm too old to walk away and find love, but you are not."

I cried like a baby when she was talking because I knew that she knew exactly what I had gone through. I let her know that I loved her too. I also told her that when she was ready to leave, she could stay with me or I would help her get her own place. She just smiled and told me that she loved me.

Levi came over once she walked away. He got a napkin and dried my tears. He said "what have I told you about all of that crying? You are too beautiful to be crying."

I said, "you're right I do look fine tonight" and slapped him on the shoulder. He hugged me and we went back over to join the crowd. After dinner was over, we all went our separate ways. When I got home, Derrick was there sitting on the stoop. I don't have time for this shit right now. I just want to shower and go to bed.

When I got out of the car he stood and waited for me to come to the door. He handed me the flowers that he had been holding in his hand. He apologized for his behavior during his last visit to my house. He asked if he could come in and talk. I allowed him to come in but told him I could only give him fifteen minutes of my time. That seemed to piss him off, but he didn't say anything.

We came into the house and went to the kitchen. I put on a fresh pot of coffee and then sat down at the table. I allowed him to begin the conversation since he wanted to talk. Of course, he said the usual; "Marie I'm sorry, I never meant to hurt you. I love you and I don't want a divorce. I am going to counseling for my sex addition." I looked up shocked Derrick get the fuck out! You don't have a dam sex addiction you are just a dog! There is no us and there will never be us again. This only angered him more.

My phone began to ring, and I knew it was Levi because I had not called him once I returned home. Derrick looked at me and his eyes became dark" That better not be your punk ass boyfriend calling you this time of night."

"First off, I am too old to have a boyfriend. Second, that is my friend Levi calling to make sure that I made it home safely. And third, before I could get the words out of my mouth Derrick had slapped me.

He began to choke me and say "No other man will ever have you. You are mine and mine only!" I didn't know who this man was that was standing in front of me. All I could do was beg for my life. I told him if I didn't answer, Levi would continue to call me. He began to beat me. As he was beating me, he said "If I let you live do you think that your man will want a cripple bitch."

At that time, I didn't know what he would do to me. I started backing out then I felt his lips on mine. Then he started rubbing on my breast. I couldn't believe that this fool had beaten me and now he is trying to have sex with me. All he said "was look what you made me do! 'The tears burned my skin as I began to cry more. I let things get this far!

My phone rang again then I heard someone yelling my name from outside my front door. It felt like hours, but I heard the door rattling and Levi and Trent bust through the door. When they saw me lying on the floor beaten and bruised Trent walked over to tend to me, and Levi went after Derrick. I pleaded with Trent to get Levi because it wasn't worth it. I could tell that Trent was pissed with me, but I couldn't let Levi go to jail because of my stupidity.

He walked over and grabbed Levi off Derrick. Trent didn't know that I saw him kick Derrick in his ribs. While Levi was beating him, he kept yelling I love you Marie. Once everything was calmed down the girls walked in. Miracle saw me lying on the couch and she went livid on Derrick. She couldn't believe that her brother had turned into their father.

Miracle came over to me and apologized for Derrick's behavior. She said "I never thought he would stoop this low. We cried together as she held me. Everyone stood back and allowed us this time together. I thanked everyone and told them they could all go home. Miracle and Regina stated they were not leaving me tonight. By this time Trent had gone to his car to get his medical bag. He said that once I took my shower, he would check my wounds again and bandage me up.

Miracle and Regina walked me upstairs. Miracle ran me a warm bath and helped me bathe while Regina got my night clothes together. Once I was dressed Trent came in and checked on me and gave me something for the pain. Thank God nothing was broken. I was just in pain and bruised. But most importantly my spirit was bruised.

The girls and I talked until I fell asleep.

The next morning when I got up from the bed, I saw a figure lying at the foot of my bed. I quietly got up and turned on the bathroom light to see who it was. It was Levi! He hadn't left last night. I checked the other rooms and saw that Regina and Miracle were still sleeping. Then I walked downstairs to start breakfast and saw Trent lying on the couch and Romeo was in the kitchen already making breakfast for everyone. I was shocked to see him because I knew he was on a business trip.

"Good Morning Romeo!"

"Good Morning Marie! How are you feeling this morning?"

"I feel like I have been run over by a truck."

"I'm sorry I wasn't here last night for you."

"It's ok Romeo, it is not your problem its mine."

"Well Marie that is where you are wrong. Levi must not have told you that you ladies are now our problem."

I just laughed and asked him how he got home so fast. Regina told me that you were going to be gone for a month.

"You're right I was going to be away for a month but when Regina called last night crying, I got on the first thing smoking."

"I'm happy that she has you in her life now."

"And I'm happy to be in her life." "So, tell me what's going on with you and Levi."

"Levi and I are just friends."

"With a smirk on his face Romeo said; "The he almost killed your husband over you last night type of friend."

"He didn't almost kill Derrick but yes we are friends. No, we are not in a relationship if that is what you are fishing for. As you can see by last night I have too much going on to even think about being with someone."

"Well, all I am going to say is this, Levi is a good man and any woman that would have him will be happy for the rest of her life. He is the one that keeps all of us grounded. He is just an all-around good dude."

"I know that Levi is a good man and the fact that he would be good for me but I'm still finding me."

"Marie just know that you were never lost. You might have let yourself go and catered to a fool but in order to still be standing you never lost you. You just put you on the back burner. You gave all of you to a man that didn't deserve it. Most women know that a man doesn't deserve their love, but they will give it willingly. Giving this type of man your love is damaging to your soul, heart and mind. Regina told me how the two of you met. That tells me that you stayed with Derrick thinking you could change him. Just know this; he only stayed with you because he knew that you would be a good woman to have on his arms. Although you might have complained you would still be there to clean up his mess. He never gave two shits about you! If he did, he would have treated you like the delicate flower you are. I'm saying all of this to say this, don't let the things that he has done tarnish your view on love. Every man or woman is not the same."

While he was speaking, I sat at the table and began to cry. Everything that he said is true. Romeo came over to comfort me and he began to silently pray. I have never had a strong male role model in life like these three men that surround me today.

As he says amen, I hear Levi say, "get your hands off my woman"! By this time the girls are downstairs, and Trent is also walking into the kitchen. Everyone laughs as Romeo throws his hands in the air in defeat

Levi says "That's what I thought, now go over there with your woman. I'm sure she is happy to see you." Levi hugs me and I mouthed to Romeo "thank you".

Everyone has concerned eyes on me now. "Are you ok? They all say in unison?

I let them all know that I am feeling better; I just need to get ready for work.

"Work!" Regina and Miracle yelled.

"Yes, I am going to work. I just started this job yesterday. My face isn't bad a little extra makeup will cover up the bruises."

I could tell that Levi was concerned about me.

We all sat down and had the delicious breakfast that Romeo cooked. We made the plan to meet back here for dinner.

When I went upstairs to get ready there was a knock on my door. I yelled "just a minute". When I got to the door it was Levi. He asked could he come in so he could talk to me. When he entered the room, he stood there for a moment staring at me.

"Marie you are so beautiful!'

I smiled then put my head down.

Levi reached out and lifted my head. He said "Don't ever put your head down when I say that you are beautiful. Just because your husband could not appreciate you don't mean that another man can't."

We walked over to the bed and he says: "I want you to pack a bag and stay with

Miracle for a couple days." All I could say was thank you for your concern, but I will be staying in my own home.

"Ok, if that is how you want it.

"It's not how I want it but how it is."

"Marie, I know that you are scared."

"Levi just leave it alone! I am staying in my own home and that is final."

"For now, I will!"

He walks out of the room; turns and looks at me. He didn't utter a word. I could tell that this was not over and that I would not win.

I walked in the bathroom showered, did my makeup and you couldn't tell that there were any bruises on my face. I dressed and walked down stairs, and everyone was waiting for me. I grabbed my purse and my brief case, but I couldn't find my keys. At that moment Levi walked back in the house and said "you're not driving to work today. Just consider me your chauffer for today." Inside I was laughing because he had balls but, on the outside, I was fuming. Everyone turned their heads as if they didn't know what was going on. One by one they all began to leave. I never thought to ask where the heck my keys were.

Miracle and Regina hugged me and said they would be by for lunch today. Romeo and Trent said they would stop by to check on me later. That only left Levi and I standing in the house staring each other down. Levi said, "This is a battle that I will not lose Marie, just get your ass in the car and stop being so damn stubborn."

Before I could respond Miracle called. She said "I know you will fuss at me later, but I took your keys.

You have no choice now but to either ride with Levi or stay home from work. If you stay home, you know Levi will be there all day." She laughed and hung up the phone. If she was in front of me, I would choke the shit out of her.

Levi opened the door and said "Right this way my lady" with a smirk on his face.

He checked all the doors and made sure everything was locked up. We rode to my job in silence. When we pulled up in front of my office, he grabbed my hand and began to pray.

"Father we come to you this morning thanking you for our health and strength. We come asking that you continue to work on our bodies, our spirits and our mind. Lord we ask that you continue to be a covering over our family and friends. Let my life be a continuous testimony as it may help others that are going through the things You have already taken me through. Father I ask that you keep your stronghold over Marie. Give her strength where she is weak. Continue to guide her feet in the direction that you will have her to go. Bless her today Lord that she can make it through today without distractions. We ask this in Your Name Lord, Amen. I got out of the car feeling a relief of the pressure that I had been carrying since my altercation with Derrick. All I could say was "Lord let Thy will be done."

When I walked into the building, I saw Kami standing there staring out of the window. She asked if that was my husband. I asked how she knew I was married because I never mentioned it. She pointed to my wedding rings. I looked at her and said, "No that's not my husband he is just a good friend of mine." She looked at me strangely and said "oh, does your husband know that your good friend is dropping you off at work." "If it is any of your concern; no, he doesn't! I have issues going on in my life that I care not to discuss at work."

CHAPTER 16

Working at this advertising company is really going to help me build my portfolio. Being that it is an internship I am forced to work as a stripper at night. I strip to take care of the four children I never had. Better yet just say I have five children since I take care of everybody. My mother is a woman who lives beyond her means. She gets government assistance for all her children. She lives in section 8 housing and she get one thousand dollars a month in food stamps. For each child the government gives her two hundred and fifty dollars plus a utility check to maintain her household. Unfortunately, with all this assistance there is never any food in the house. The children don't have clothes. The house is nasty. I try my best to be a good person, but life hasn't been easy for me. I didn't sign up to be a mother.

While I'm at the strip club every night shaking my ass, my mother is somewhere laying on her back getting fucked or with a dick in her mouth. When I get home, she has her hand out asking for money. If I don't give it to her she would just beat me and take it from me. My mother didn't care anything for us we were just a check to her. If she was a real mother, my thirteen-year-old sister wouldn't be pregnant right now. There have been several months that I had to fuck and suck the landlord not to be evicted because Joy didn't pay the rent. I am not sure why the checks came to her and not directly to the landlord. When I told my mother what I had to do she said, "that's what a good bitch would do".

So instead of fucking the landlord every month I would strip to make the money. Little did I know I would be selling my ass at the strip club too that is until I met this man named Derrick. He was a regular at the club. Sometimes he would come in with other men and have dinner. I later found out that those were business meetings. After watching me for several months he asked for a private dance. He knew what was going on in those back rooms. I had seen him go back there a few times with a stripper named Icy. Once we got in the back, I danced for him. I was surprised that he didn't want any sexual favors. Turns out he just wanted to talk. Derrick told me that he could see that something was bothering me, and he just wanted to be of help any way that he could. I laughed it off and danced for him. I knew that he wanted something from me.

Derrick came back several times and eventually invited me out on a date. Honestly, I had never been on a date and didn't know what to expect. I accepted his invitation. Later that week we went out for dinner. The food and the conversation were good. I had never had a guy take interest in me unless it was for sexual favors. He really treated me like a woman. I told him that I was twenty and had never really had a boyfriend. Derrick laughed and said, "well you do now."

After that night we were inseparable. I later found out months after dating, that he was married. It was too late to leave him because my heart was already invested in the relationship. He told me that his wife was refusing to give him a divorce. Things with them had been over but she wouldn't let go. I don't know how women could be so stupid. If the man doesn't want, you why are you still holding on? I always thought his wife was a lonely bitter fat bitch sitting at home mad all the time. She must have been stupid because we spent many days and nights together in their apartment. When my mother found out about our relationship all she said was "Yo ass betta not be fucking for free! There is a cost for everything." She knew that he was much older than me, but she didn't care. All she wanted was the money.

Derrick made me happy. The money that I made stripping I still spent making sure my siblings were ok. However, he made sure I had everything that I asked for. Being with him upgraded my style. He told me that if I was going to be seen with him in public, I couldn't wear thrift store cloth any longer. I went to a couple business luncheons with him. He showed me the kind of world that I could live in if I completed college.

Derrick wrote my recommendation to get my current internship. Once I prove myself, I will be able to get a paid internship at the company.

For the past couple of months Derrick has been acting strange. He only calls me when he wants sex. There have been several times that he has come to my job on lunch; not to take me to eat but to get his dick sucked. For some reason he has started treating me like some common whore and I don't like it. Last night he called me crying because he had been in a bar fight. I stayed up all night and nursed his wounds. Even through his pain he found me sexy.

Last night was the first time ever that he ever told me that he loved me. A lone tear dropped from my eyes. No one has ever told me that they loved me not even my mother. I kissed him as he winced in pain. I dropped down to my knees and attempted to suck his dick. Something was wrong because nothing happened. He said Marie just come lay with me. At first, I was pissed but there are times that he would call me that. That was his pet name for me because it was a mature name. The name was befitting to me and my personality.

CHAPTER 17

After I dropped Marie off at work, I made a quick detour to talk to my pastor. He was also a friend of mine. I pulled up at Pastor Jay's house and sat in my car for a few minutes. I was contemplating pulling off when I heard a tap on the window. I looked up and was greeted by Jay Jr.

"Hi Mr. Levi, How are you today Sir?"

Hey Jr. I'm good. I haven't seen you and the boys at the gym lately. Everything alright?

"Yes, everything is fine. I just need to spend less time working out and more time in the books."

I understand. If you need help with anything you know I'm just a phone call away.

"I know, and thanks. Gotta go! Dad is in his office waiting for you."

When I walked into the office Pastor Jay gave me a huge man hug. He then asked how I was doing. I told him about my friendship with Marie. I talked about the difficult time that she is having with her soon to be ex-husband. We talked about the developing feelings that I have for her. He was happy for me. He told me that he knows that she's the light in my eyes that use to be there before my wife and child died. The words that he spoke only made me a little more confused when I left than I was when I came in.

He said "Levi, God places people in our lives for a time and a season. Bridgette came into your life to teach you how to love selflessly. God doesn't make mistakes. Marie being in your life now is His way of releasing all the hurt that the both of you are carrying. She needs more time to figure out her life. See the loss of your wife was a physical lost; Marie is facing a mental lost. Be patient with her."

I left the pastor's house with a refresh mind. I called Trent and Romeo to make sure that they would have everything in place for the ladies tonight. Trent informed me that he was going to be late due to an emergency surgery that he had to perform. Romeo was already at Marie's house with Regina cooking dinner. Today we would all get to meet Nyla, the young lady that she has with Derrick.

When I got to Marie's job, she was standing outside talking to a young woman. I later found out that was her assistant by the name of Kami. She was out there also waiting on her ride. Her boyfriend was late to pick her up. We offered her a ride, but she declined.

We made it to the house within thirty minutes. Romeo and Regina were in the kitchen putting the finishing touches on dinner. Regina baked my favorite chocolate cake. Romeo made grilled steaks, loaded bake potatoes, asparagus and a green salad. We all talked to each other about our days and every doted over Nyla. That night she stayed under me more than usual. I am not sure if she could sense something was wrong or not. Regina yelled of course because she says Marie always spoils Nyla whenever she is around. I keep trying to get her to understand that she is the daughter I would never have.

Nyla says "ok Ma'rie, I must go in the other room now. I don't want to make momma mad". As she walked out of the room she mouthed "I like when you spoil me, that's why you are my Ma'rie". Seeing Marie's interaction with little Nyla made me long for my lost child. Nyla knows that She is not her mother, but she calls her Ma'rie since she was married to her father. She says Ma and then added the last part of her first name, Ma'rie!

I stuck out my tongue to Regina and the guys laughed. Miracle said, "you two children stop it now before I swat you." This really made the guys laugh. At that very moment Trent walked in looking tired. Miracle got up from the table and fixed his plate. Once she sat his plate on the table she hugged and kissed him. I am happy that my brothers are finally finding happiness. I may not be in a relationship yet with Marie, but she truly makes me happy.

After dinner we all sat around and talked. I could tell that Marie was getting tired, so I told everyone that it was time to leave. Miracle looked at me and asked if I told her yet. Marie was looking confused, tell me what. Regina got up and hugged me. She whispered in my ear to take care of her sister. As she was walking to the door Romeo was coming down the stairs with a sleeping Nyla. I walked over to the front door and bided everyone goodnight. I walked back over to the couch grabbed my book and sat down. Marie was still looking confused.

She said, "What the hell do you think you are doing?"

"Remember the conversation we had this morning about you being safe."

"Yes, and I told you that I was fine!"

"No, you refused to go and stay somewhere else until all of this shit calms down. So, since you won't leave, I will stay. I will not fight you over this. I will stay either in the house or on your front porch. You just tell me where you want me."

"Fine! Do whatever it is that you want."

CHAPTER 18

Marie

When Levi decided to stay the night to protect me, I was flattered. Being around Levi does things to my body that has not happened in a very long time. How the hell am I supposed to sleep knowing that this fine ass man is in the next room.

I went upstairs showered and prepared for the next day. Once I got into bed there was a knock on my door.

"Come in!"

Levi walked in with a cup of chamomile tea. This man is so thoughtful. Whatever woman let him go should be ashamed. I smiled and said thank you. He kissed me on the forehead and said, "Goodnight my beauty!" 'Feeling his lips on my skin only made me desire him more. I have not had sex in months. I have not been this attracted to a man since the early stages of my relationship with Derrick.

That night I tossed and turned thinking of Levi. I thought about what my life would be like. Knowing that he was in the next room drove me crazy. After several hours of contemplating going to his room naked, I pulled out my gifts from Miracle. It was a wireless double silver bullet with several speeds and a nine-inch dildo. When she gave them to me, I threw them in the back of the drawer. I never planned on using any of it. Levi being here has changed that.

I pushed the covers off me then tossed my night gown to the floor. My skin felt warm as I began to rub on myself. I could hear that old Tweet song playing in my head. I turned myself on so much I thought there was a man in there with me. I started to play with myself using only my hand until I was wet. Once I was wet enough, I placed the bullet on my clitoris. I started the speed out on low and as I increased the speed, I inserted the dildo. Before I knew it, I was climaxing. I pushed the dildo deeper inside me as I rubbed on my breast. The fire that was burning in me would not let me stop. I kept going, cuming over and over again all while calling out Levi's name. The next thing I knew, Levi was busting through my door. I was just as shocked as he was seeing me lying there naked with my dildo hanging out my pussy and my fingers on my clitoris. I couldn't say anything, and neither could he. He stood there and stared at me for what seemed like eternity before turning around and walking out the door.

That next morning, I didn't want to face him. When I walked down the stairs, he was sitting at the kitchen table eating his breakfast and reading the morning paper. He looked up from reading the paper to let me know that my plate was in the microwave. I couldn't bear to look at him. When I sat down to the table he apologized for bursting into my room in the middle of the night. He heard me scream his name and thought I needed him. I did need him, but I will never say it to him. I accepted his apology and we got ready for the gym. This morning I was going into work late in order to take some self-defense classes. When I got to the class, I bumped into my boss Stephanie.

"Hi Stephanie!"

"Hi Marie, I didn't know you take this class."

This is my first time taking the class. Due to some unfortunate circumstances in my life, my friends think it is necessary.

"Well that is the same reason I started taking the classes a year ago. After an incident with my now ex-husband, my friends were scared to leave me alone."

"Same here, my friends should be coming in soon. I'll make sure to introduce you."

"Great let's get started!"

The class was an hour long and I am truly exhausted. I introduced Stephanie to Regina and Miracle. I told her that I would see her in the office later today. But Regina offered her to come shopping and to lunch with us. She looked at me for acceptance. I told her it was ok. We left the gym and went to the mall to shop for our upcoming getaway. Once we were done shopping, we went to Olive Garden for lunch. At lunch we got to know more about Stephanie and her ex-husband. It looks like Stephanie will become a part of our sister circle. She just moved here and has no one.

I told the girls what happed last night with Levi. Miracle laughed so hard that she started crying. Regina had a look of shock on her face and Stephanie wanted to know why I didn't fuck him when he walked into the room. She was going to fit in great with the ladies.

CHAPTER 19

Levi

It took all the willpower I had not to jump in that bed with Marie last night. It's true that I am falling for her, but I am waiting for her to see her own value. Once she can see the value in herself then she will be free to come to me.

I am the type of man that is looking for a wife. I don't need a girlfriend or a plaything. I'm too old for toys and games. I will patiently wait until God says it is time. Each day I pray for her healing. I want Marie to see what I see when I look at her. When I look at her, I can see the broken little girl in her eyes

CHAPTER 20

It has been a couple months since I have heard from Derrick. I know that he has gone back to that bitch of a wife of his. I will give him until next month to come back home. The way that he treated me the last time we were together has already been forgiven. I love this man and I refuse to lose him to a woman that doesn't know how to truly love him.

I need to let him know that I am pregnant again with our second baby. This time I know he will marry me. I know that he is ok because all the bills are paid, and money is being added to the account to take care of necessities. I just can't figure out why he isn't calling me back. Why hasn't he been home to see me or his son? The daycare has let me know that he has dropped by there a couple times this week. I just need to call him one more time.

As I am calling him, I pray that he answers the phone. Of course, he doesn't answer so I leave a message. Baby please come home, we miss you. Whatever I did to make you shut me out I'm sorry. I have already forgiven you for having sex with me in that manner. I know that it was my fault and I will never do it again. Please just come home!

I know he won't call me back. I have to let him know where I stand. I can't lose Derrick.

By the next day Derrick still had not retuned my call. I went over to his precious Marie's house to make him come home. I took Jr. with me to make him talk to me. He will never raise his voice at me in front of his son.

It took a while for someone to answer the door. When they finally opened the door, I couldn't speak. The lady asked if she could help me with something. She then looked down at my son and knew exactly who I was.

"What the hell are you doing here?"

"I am here to see you about Derrick."

"Derrick is my brother so why would you want to see me. I don't have anything to do with him."

"Is Derrick here?"

"If he was, I wouldn't tell you with your home wrecking ass!"

"Look I don't want to play games with you. Is Derrick here or not? If he is not, I need to speak with his ex-wife Marie."

"You mean his wife Marie?"

"Whatever, is she home?"

At that moment another woman came to the door and she asked me if she could help me. I told her I was looking for Marie.

She said, "I'm Marie, how may I help you?"

I reached out my hand to shake hers and both women just looked at me." Hi, I'm Diane and I am looking for Derrick".

"Well Derrick is not here nor is he welcomed to come here."

"If you don't want him here, why won't you divorce him then?"

"First any questions you have about my soon to be ex-husband you need to ask him. But since you seem to be misinformed let me help you out. Derrick has gotten the papers three months ago but has refused to sign them. When you see him please ask him to sign the divorce papers. Once he does, he is all yours. And don't worry I don't ever want him back. He is a headache you can keep."

I stood there dumbfounded as the door was being closed in my face. As I was walking back to my car there was a car pulling up. One of the guys in the car looked familiar. When they got out of the car, I recognized it was Trent. When I saw him, my body began to tremble. I can't believe I'm still afraid of this man.

Trent got out of the car and walked over to me when he recognized who I was. The first question he asked was if that was his son. I told him no. He looked different than the last time I saw him. He was a more distinguished man now. It was something about him that made me smile although I was still afraid. Trent leaned over and hugged me and said it was good to see me. He has yet to apologize for anything that he did to me.

I left Marie's house wondering why the hell Trent was there and where the hell was Derrick? When I got home, I dropped Derrick Jr. off at daycare and decided to do a little shopping. Maybe if I fix myself up Derrick would appreciate me more. I know you might not understand why I refuse to let go of this man. He is my saving grace and he is all that I have in life besides my son. As you know life for me has not been easy. I refuse to be out on the streets again. Derrick has given me the life that I have always wanted and deserved. Being with him has been a calming experience to my life. Imagining my life without him would be like committing suicide.

COMING SOON!

Beautifully Broken

PROLOGUE

Diane's Story

Growing up never feeling love from the people that were supposed to love me ruined my image on life and relationships. Being a product of rape, growing up feeling unwanted and being told that I was nothing, but trash caused me to have a horrible self-image of myself.

My mother losing her first love because of my conception caused me to fester in hate inside of her during her pregnancy. See my mother was raped by her boyfriend's high school teammate. When my father returned from basic training and found my mom pregnant, he rejected her. She tried to explain the rape, but he had already been informed by his teammate that he had slept with my mother willing. This left my mother devastated and made her hate me because I was the cause of her greatest loss.

When I was born my mother refused to touch me or even look at me. She hated me from the day that he left her, Junior was her way out of this shitty town. When he joined the military, she knew he would give her the life that she deserved. The rape ruined all of her hopes and dreams which made her give up on everything. All her anger and frustrations were turned to me as I was the cause of everything bad that had and will happen in her life.

My grandmother decided to raise me on her own. Life with Odessa wasn't easy. She was old and didn't want to be bothered with any children. She treated me like trash. As a baby she made sure I was feed, dry and had on clean clothes nothing more. She only interacted with me when we had company over or in public. During these times she was the perfect grandmother.

I grew up expecting to be treated bad. I saw my grandmother get beat by my mother's father. Earl only came around at the 1st of each month. We would have a little family outing but later that night he would turn into the devil. He would pick a fight with my grandmother and beat her when he felt like she had gotten out of line then leave. When he left my grandmother mentally and physically broken. I did all that I could to clean her up. I always asked. "Grandma, why do you allow Mr. Earl to treat you like this?" She would just say that I would understand when I got older.

As I got older, I yearned for the love that I never received. Odessa did the best that she could to show me love, I guess. You already know that I got nothing but hate from my mom. I'd seen what love looked like on television and in the movies but never in real life. Everyone around me was suffering from something in their relationships.

www.ingramcontent.com/pod-product-compliance
Lightning Source LLC
Chambersburg PA
CBHW070756280626
47162CB00016B/1156